GLADIATOR'S EMBRACE

IMPERIAL GAMES, BOOK 1

JENNA BIGELOW

Content Warning

This book contains depictions of combat violence, murder, slavery, grief, and attempted sexual assault.

1

Ferox tipped several silver coins into his hand from the leather bag. They gleamed against his scarred palm, more money than he'd seen in a long time. The coins would show their age soon, as they still bore the image of the recently deceased emperor Tiberius, rather than the new one. But that didn't make them worth any less.

"A hundred thousand sestertii?" Ferox repeated, sure he'd heard the figure wrong amid the noise of the bustling tavern. That was as much as a skilled, educated man would make in a *year*. And Lucullus was offering him that for three fights in two months?

His former manager, seated across from him at the table, nodded. Lucullus was a diminutive man of middle age whose even-handed manner held the respect of every man in his ludus. "That bag contains the first thousand, as a deposit. The rest will be paid after each match. Thirty thousand after each of the first two fights. Forty thousand for the last. Plus additional prize money, at Gaius Caesar's pleasure."

The numbers tangled themselves up in Ferox's mind. "And that adds up to a hundred thousand?"

Another nod from Lucullus. Ferox trusted him; during the decade that Ferox had been fighting for Lucullus's ludus, their dealings had always been honest and fair, despite the fact that until recently, the manager had owned him.

Ferox stared at the coins, imagining that amount a hundred times over. Life had been hard since walking away from the arena eighteen months ago. His position at the ludus offered a stability he'd learned not to take for granted, even though he hadn't chosen this life. He probably never would have left, if not for Hector's death.

But his best friend had died because of him, and leaving seemed like the only way to get some relief from the ghost that haunted him.

"I've seen many men leave," Lucullus said. "Or try to. Not easy, is it?"

Ferox made a reluctant noise of agreement. He'd scraped together enough money to buy his freedom and left with barely a sestertius to his name. He had no skill except fighting, and only the most rudimentary education.

He'd managed to pick up jobs here and there as a guard, trading on his imposing size and reputation. Plenty of powerful men—senators, other politicians, businessmen—wanted to be seen with a famous gladiator like Ferox in their entourage, and they paid well enough, but Ferox tried to avoid those jobs. His reduced circumstances were embarrassing, and he hated feeling like he was on display. He preferred working for merchants who needed security as they transported their goods to Ostia, Tibur, or other nearby cities. That work at least made him useful, providing an opportunity to use the skills and strength he'd honed over nearly fifteen years of fighting.

Still, more often than not, he'd gone to bed hungry, cursing the circumstances that had led him to abandon the closest thing he had to a home. There was something to be said for knowing where his next meal was coming from, for having a safe place to rest his head at night.

But Hector's death had changed everything. Victory in the arena no longer held any pleasure for him, and he couldn't face his two remaining friends without knowing he was the reason Hector had died.

Ferox swept the coins back into the bag, hiding them from view of any too-curious onlookers. "Gaius Caesar is truly offering this much? For me?"

Lucullus nodded. "He wants to host the greatest games the city's ever seen to celebrate his accession. He seeks all the best gladiators, even the retired ones. When his representative came to see me, he asked specifically for you."

A touch of pride flared at the thought that the young emperor, now the most powerful man in the world, knew his name. "He's the one they call…what was it? Little Shoe?"

A wrinkle appeared between Lucullus's gray brows. "Little Boots, I believe."

Ah, right. Ferox remembered hearing a tale of how the new emperor had earned the nickname *Caligula*: the result of a childhood spent in his late father's military camps, dressed in a child's version of an army uniform, complete with miniature legionary boots.

"But I would not speak that name too loudly, if I were you," Lucullus continued. "No man wishes to be reminded of his childhood nickname. Especially not an emperor."

Ferox grunted in acknowledgement. He couldn't argue with that.

"The games will last eight weeks," Lucullus said. "You'll fight in three matches, as I've said, and you'll keep any winnings in addition to the hundred thousand."

Three matches. A hundred thousand sestertii, plus winnings. That much money could truly give him a fresh start at anything he chose. He could finally return to Hispania, his homeland, and forge a new life of peace and stability. He could buy a vineyard, or a farm, or invest in a mine, something profitable that would see money in his coffers without having to toil for it. Not that he knew anything about vineyards or farms or mines, but with that much money, he could hire people who did.

"Three final fights," Lucullus pressed, his voice taking on that persuasive note that Ferox remembered well. "It's a once-in-a-lifetime deal. You know it is."

Ferox wanted to refuse, to turn his back on the money. Coming back to the ludus would force him to face the ghosts he'd been fleeing. But rejecting an offer like this would mean more hungry nights and days spent feeling like a failure. Lucullus was offering him a second chance, a way to secure his future once and for all.

"Fine," he growled.

A broad smile spread over Lucullus's weathered face. "Excellent." He tossed down a few bronze coins to pay for their wine. "I'll have your old room cleaned out. Gather your things and come tonight. Training starts tomorrow. In three weeks, the games begin." He bid Ferox goodbye with a nod, then left the tavern.

Ferox tied the bag of coin tight. Another man might be nervous to walk the streets carrying a sum of this magnitude, but Ferox's reputation meant thieves and brigands gave him a wide berth. Even so, he wasn't about to flash the money carelessly.

He rose to his feet, bag grasped in his fist, and navigated the maze of tables and stools to find the exit. Despite the fortune that awaited him, his decision weighed heavy in his gut. Returning meant giving himself over to the guilt he'd been trying desperately to keep at bay. But for two months, he could weather it.

Three more fights. Then he would truly be free.

As twilight shadows stretched, Ferox made his way back to the ludus, the walled complex of buildings where Lucullus's gladiators lived and trained. The guard at the entrance recognized him and hastily straightened up.

"So it's true!" the guard spluttered. "You really are back."

Ferox passed through the gate without response. He was not interested in entertaining everyone's surprise that he'd returned. There were only two people here whose opinion he cared about, and he hoped they wouldn't gloat too much at his return.

A gray-brown shadow darted in front of Ferox at ankle height. He stopped in his tracks. "Still alive, are you?" he said to the yellow-eyed cat.

Nyx put his ragged ears flat against his striped head and hissed, then ran away, disappearing into the dusk.

That was the welcome Ferox had anticipated from the ludus's infamously ill-tempered resident cat.

A deep voice materialized from the gloom. "I could ask the same of you."

Ferox glanced up to see the rangy form of Jason, leaning against the wall of the nearest building.

Unlike with Nyx, Ferox wasn't sure what sort of reception to expect from Jason, one of his two remaining friends. After all, he hadn't exactly upheld his promise to stay in touch after leaving the ludus a year and a half ago.

Jason slunk closer. "Lucullus said you were coming back. I said there was no way. He must have gotten you confused with another thick-headed, surly ex-gladiator."

Ferox glowered at him, but the scowl on Jason's face lasted for only another moment before splitting into a grin. Jason let out a ringing chuckle and punched Ferox in the shoulder. "Is it true he offered you a hundred thousand sestertii for three measly fights? Dis, that's ridiculous. Come, let's find your room. I doubt you remember the way after all this time." He gave Ferox a good-natured eye-roll and beckoned him further into the ludus.

The complex was arranged as a cluster of buildings that surrounded a large open field used for training. A sturdy wall enclosed the ludus, meant to keep curious fans out and gladiators in, though veteran fighters were trusted to go about the city as they pleased during their free time. The buildings housed kitchens, storerooms, privies, a laundry, a dining hall, and barracks.

Alongside Jason, Ferox entered the long, narrow barracks building. It housed rows of doors that led to cell-like bedrooms. The doors latched from both the inside and the outside—though the outer locks were only used if a new gladiator was deemed an escape risk.

They reached his old room; despite Jason's joke, Ferox did remember where it was. A wall lamp had been lit, which cast a flickering light over the sparse surroundings. The room was as small as Ferox recalled, barely wide enough for a man as tall as himself to stretch out his arms without brushing the walls on both sides. But the floor was swept clean, and the narrow bed bore fresh linens.

On that bed, a dark-haired woman sat cross-legged, swathed in a loose dress. Penthesilea, one of the few female gladiators in the city and the only one in Lucullus's ludus, surveyed him with as much disdain as Nyx. "Welcome back, old man."

"It's good to see you too, Lea." He was only a few years older than Jason and Lea, but for a gladiator, reaching the age of thirty made him practically ancient.

She narrowed her eyes at him, but he didn't miss the twitch of her lips—a hastily suppressed smile. "Your room has some new graffiti, I'm afraid." She beckoned to the wall next to his bed.

Ferox raised his eyebrows as he caught sight of the graffiti. The paint appeared suspiciously fresh, and the writing looked like Lea's clumsy hand.

It took him a few moments to parse the uneven letters. *Ferox the gladiator has the smallest cock in the* ~~city~~ *empire.* Beneath was an artful sketch of a burly, armored gladiator expertly fellating a monstrous disembodied penis.

"Your portfolio is expanding, I see," Ferox said to Jason, who enjoyed sketching in his spare time.

Jason gave a self-satisfied grin. "It's my finest work, no doubt."

"Good luck getting a woman into your bed now," Lea added with a smug head-tilt at the graffiti.

The most effort Ferox had previously expended to get a woman into his bed involved an exchange of coin, and somehow he didn't think the average courtesan would be put off by some rude graffiti.

Before he could tell Lea as much, a throat cleared behind them. Lucullus stood in the doorway.

"I see you've found your chamber." Lucullus glanced at the graffiti with an unamused frown.

Ferox stepped out to join Lucullus in the hallway, as the room was not big enough for four. As he did so, he noticed an unfamiliar young woman at Lucullus's shoulder. Women were an uncommon sight within the walls of the ludus, except for servants, the occasional courtesan, and Penthesilea. This newcomer certainly wasn't Lea, and he'd never known Lucullus to bring a woman to the ludus. But nor did she have the bearing of a servant.

In the dimness of the corridor, it was hard to see her face clearly, but Ferox could make out a messy braid of curly, wheat-colored hair that laid over her shoulder. A linen dress swathed her from shoulder to ankle, and her figure beneath it was small and delicate. He guessed she was in her early twenties, perhaps eight or ten years younger than himself.

Lucullus handed over a piece of papyrus, recalling Ferox's attention from the woman he couldn't place. "This records our agreement, and the terms of your three payments."

Ferox took the paper and nodded. "Thank you." He didn't bother trying to read the clusters of words. If Lucullus said the paper recorded those things, Ferox believed him.

The woman's eyes ran over him with brazen interest. Usually, female attention was couched behind a veneer of coyness. This woman, however, examined him so thoroughly he felt as if her sharp gaze was burning straight through the worn fabric of his tunic.

He caught her gaze, expecting her to flinch in embarrassment at having been caught staring. Instead, she just smiled at him, her manner assured and utterly unabashed.

Lucullus noticed his focus and placed a hand on the young woman's shoulder. "Ah, I forgot you won't have met Velia, my niece. She joined me here a year ago. She's become a trusted assistant."

Ferox nodded to her. He couldn't help wondering how in Hades Lucullus's niece had ended up working for him here, of all places. *How does a young woman find herself working at a ludus?*

Velia returned his acknowledgement, then glanced at the graffiti, just visible through the open door. "I can have someone whitewash that for you," she offered. Then her eyebrows arched. "Unless you prefer to, well, under-promise and over-deliver?"

Behind Ferox, Jason snorted.

The pert insinuation in her words made a discomfiting heat rise to his face. Thankfully, the light was dim. "Leave it," he grunted, affecting carelessness. "A bit of graffiti doesn't bother me." His name was scrawled all over the city in various contexts—usually flattering, but not always—and he'd long ago learned to ignore that sort of notoriety.

"Very well," Velia said, a smile still playing around her lips.

"Training starts tomorrow morning," Lucullus said. "I trust you remember the schedule?"

Ferox nodded. He'd be woefully out of practice, no doubt, so the first few days would be grueling, but he had to put in the work if he didn't want to dishonor himself in his first match.

Lucullus left, and Velia followed after casting Ferox one last curious glance. Lea and Jason also returned to their own rooms with a promise to see him tomorrow for breakfast, leaving Ferox alone.

He sat heavily on his bed, staring at the blank wall opposite him. This was always where he used to feel Hector's ghost the strongest, when he was in this room by himself at night. Ferox closed his eyes, extending his senses. He hoped that the time elapsed since his departure might have released the shade's tether on him.

But as he sat in the darkness, a vision hit him, burning itself into the space behind his eyes: the last moments of Hector's life, a sword driving down, the deafening cheers of the crowd. Ferox's desperate helplessness as he watched.

His eyes flew open, fixating on the flame of the lamp even though the brightness hurt.

Yes, Hector was still here. Still haunting him. Still wanting to make Ferox suffer.

He'd heard of such things before, ghosts who lingered near their living relations or friends. Some were benevolent, there to watch over those they'd cared for in life. Others, not so much.

In life, Hector had been the best of men: warmhearted, generous with his jokes and smiles, somehow maintaining his goodness despite the brutal and bloody business they were all entangled in.

On its face, it wasn't so surprising that one of them had died in the arena, even though a losing gladiator was likely to be spared if he yielded. Gladiators were valuable, and though the decision depended on the whims of the audience and ultimately rested with the host of the games, the host had to pay a hefty fine to the manager of a slain gladiator.

Death, however, was still an ever-present risk. Each fight could be one's last, and Ferox had always known that sooner or later, he would mourn one of his friends or they him.

But it was different with Hector, because Ferox himself had been slated to fight that day. He'd been laid up with a minor injury, so Hector had taken his place. That was why, two years later, guilt still had its claws in him. Hector would be alive if not for him.

Even worse, Hector's opponent hadn't granted him the professional courtesy of a quick, clean end. Instead, it had been bloody, torturous, one of the most stomach-turning things Ferox had ever seen. And the crowd loved every moment.

This was the life he'd elected to return to—one where the entire city cheered to watch a man be slaughtered. That could very well be his fate if he lost any of his three fights, which was more likely than ever after so long away. He was out of shape, out of practice. Maybe he'd lost whatever spark had given him such an illustrious career. No one could fight forever. Eventually, both luck and skill ran dry. Would he even make it through his three fights?

Well, he'd find out soon enough.

2

Velia stood beneath the shaded portico as she watched the new gladiator, Ferox, train. To be fair, he wasn't exactly new—in fact, he was the most experienced in the ludus. He must be at least thirty, and his body bore the marks of a long fighting career. As he sparred with Jason, sunlight glanced off an array of scars over his bare chest and arms, and Velia bet his nose had been broken at least three times.

But his rugged appearance still drew her eye. Muscles bulged and rippled as he thrust the blunt practice sword at Jason, who nimbly caught the blow against his shield.

"What do you think of him?" her uncle Lucullus asked from where he watched beside her.

She turned her scrutiny from appreciative to assessing. "He's out of practice, but I can tell he's experienced. I see how he anticipates each move from Jason. But his footwork is clumsy, and it seems like he's finding this taxing." For all his evident strength, sweat gleamed on Ferox's forehead and shoulders, and he was breathing hard, while Jason looked as effortless as if enjoying an afternoon stroll.

"I agree." Lucullus gave an approving nod. "He's talented—there's a reason the emperor asked for him specifically—but he needs to put in the work to get back to where he once was."

Her uncle's confirmation of her opinion sent a warm flare of pride through her. If she was going to achieve her dream of managing her own troupe of gladiators one day, learning to assess their strengths and weaknesses was an essential skill.

After a year of living with her uncle at his ludus, she'd gained many skills she never knew existed. She might not be able to weave or cook to save her life, but she knew how to negotiate a gladiator's fees, maintain their weapons and equipment, and manage their diets to keep them in top fighting shape.

Lucullus left to go supervise another training match, but Velia stayed, watching Jason and Ferox spar. Jason was an animated fighter, whooping and grunting, a smile on his face with each successful hit. Ferox, on the other hand, fought with a look of grim, unwavering blankness. It didn't change, no matter if he managed a hit on Jason or took one himself.

So far, the little she had seen of him had suggested that he was perpetually in a bad mood. He seemed to communicate mostly in grunts, though he was polite to Lucullus, and she had heard him speak a full sentence to Jason and Lea as they warmed up earlier that morning. She'd caught enough of his speech to detect a slight accent, a harshness to certain consonants and an alteration to the vowels. He must be from the provinces, but she couldn't decipher his exact origin.

His manner made Velia wonder how he'd become such a revered gladiator. Gladiators weren't just fighters; they were performers. They had to win the crowd's interest, put on a show. And Ferox…well, so far, he didn't seem to have an ounce of theatrical sensibility in that huge body.

When the match ended, Ferox sat heavily on a bench at the perimeter of the training ground, wiping the sweat from his brow. His short, dark hair was plastered to his forehead.

Velia ambled over, curious to discover if she could elicit more than a grunt from him.

He ignored her as she approached the bench.

"You'll feel that tomorrow, no doubt," she said with a sympathetic smile.

His gaze flicked toward her, but he said nothing.

Maybe some flattery would soften him up. That worked on most gladiators, in her experience. "My uncle told me of your record. Twenty wins, eight draws, and three losses, right?"

"Four losses," he corrected her. Again, her ear picked up that hint of an accent.

"Four losses," she conceded. "Still, that's quite the career. Better than anyone else here." His career was most impressive in terms of sheer volume: often, gladiators didn't survive more than five or ten matches. "I'm sure it'll be twenty-three wins by the time these games are over."

"Maybe." He didn't sound particularly enthusiastic at the thought of further embellishing his record. "I get paid either way."

His nonchalance irritated her. He was supposed to be one of the greatest gladiators the city had ever seen, and he didn't even care about winning?

Sharp words rose to her tongue before she could bite them back. "Or maybe it'll be seven losses. You're huffing and puffing after one practice match as if you've climbed Mount Olympus."

Ferox's head swiveled toward her, and their gazes met. His eyes were dark, narrowed in displeasure. His brows lowered, giving the sharp planes of his face an even more forbidding appearance. Up close, she noticed a jagged scar that cut through one eyebrow.

Despite the fact that he was glaring at her as if she'd put ants in his food, a bolt of heat shot through her. A year at the ludus had shaped her into a connoisseur of the male physique, and though she would probably rate Jason the most objectively handsome of all the men, with the face and body of a temple statue, there was something about Ferox that drew her eye to linger, to savor. His size alone was impressive, but there were plenty of giants to whom she wouldn't give a second look. No, he was *handsome*—despite the scars. Despite the broken nose. Despite the glowering.

Or maybe because of all that.

"Velia!" Her uncle's voice.

She broke away from Ferox's gaze and turned to see her uncle beckoning from the other side of the training ground.

"Don't forget to stretch," she said to Ferox, then hurried away to join Lucullus.

Her uncle gestured her toward the entrance to the ludus. "There's a potential recruit I thought you might want to see."

Her interest piqued. "Really? A volunteer?"

Lucullus nodded. "Take a look. See if you think he has potential."

Since the new emperor had announced eight weeks of games to celebrate his accession, Lucullus had been hard at work recruiting or purchasing new gladiators. They needed to swell their numbers if they were going to supply enough fighters for such an extravagant display. Lucullus's agents prowled the slave markets every day in search of suitable men, and they accepted volunteers as well.

Lucullus knew of Velia's desire to manage her own troupe of gladiators, and had suggested that these games might be a good chance for her to take on her first fighter, if the right candidate presented himself. It would have to be a volunteer, rather than a slave; Velia had some money saved up from the modest wage Lucullus paid her, but not enough to finance the outright purchase of a man in addition to all the other expenses entailed in the training and upkeep of a gladiator.

Her feet sped up as she followed Lucullus. She was eager to see this volunteer. It could mean the start of everything she wanted. Her uncle had carved out a very profitable life for himself with his gladiators, and she was determined to do the same. It would mean that she'd never have to return to her family's horrible farm ever again. *This* was where she belonged, and though she didn't mind working for her uncle, she didn't plan to be just an assistant for the rest of her life. She wanted to have a hand in something great, something bigger than herself—and the games were the biggest thing she could imagine.

Lucullus led her over to a lanky man leaning against the wall just inside the entrance to the ludus. The stranger straightened up when he saw them approaching, crossing lean arms over his chest.

"Dis, that hair," Velia muttered as she took in the fiery color of his hair. A promising start: hair like that would be memorable, if nothing else.

"You want to be a gladiator?" she asked him, not waiting for her uncle to introduce them. "Why?"

He looked her over with a frown. "Well, who wouldn't?" he said, as if she'd asked if he believed the sky was blue. "Money, fame, women. Honestly, I'd expect you to have volunteers lining up from here to the Campus Martius."

They did get a trickle of volunteers, men with crushing debts or no better options to see themselves housed and fed, but the prospect of a grisly public death usually put off anyone with much of a choice.

"You know you could probably make good money selling that hair to a wigmaker." She'd only ever seen this shade of hair on the heads of patrician ladies, but they must get it from somewhere.

He made a dismissive gesture. "Tried it. Took too long to grow, and I couldn't stand looking like some sort of barbarian while it was growing out."

"Fair enough. Do you have any fighting experience? Army?" She tore her gaze from his shocking hair and evaluated the rest of his physique. He was tall but skinny. That was workable. Height couldn't be changed, but muscle could always be built.

"I've won some tavern brawls," he said, a defensive jut to his chin.

"What sort of work have you done?"

He shrugged. "Been on a few construction crews, that sort of thing."

That elucidated why he sought to become a gladiator. Despite the risk, it was probably more tolerable than a life of physical drudgery. Of course, training as a gladiator was also grueling, but it offered a chance at fame and fortune that menial jobs couldn't.

All in all, he seemed promising, which excited her. This scarlet-haired man could be her first step toward her goal.

"I want to see him fight," she announced to her uncle, who stood off to the side, watching as she questioned the man. "Can I have one of the others spar with him?" Though fighting techniques could be taught, she'd learned the best gladiators had an innate spark of talent even as complete novices.

Lucullus shook his head. "They're busy. You'll have to figure out another way to evaluate him."

"Fine." She thought for a second, then beckoned the volunteer to follow her to an unoccupied spot on the sunny training ground.

She assumed a stable stance. "Fight me." Months ago, she had wheedled Penthesilea into teaching her the basics of hand-to-hand combat, in case she should ever need to defend herself.

The man's coppery eyebrows shot up. "I'm not going to attack a *girl*."

"I want to see how you move," she pressed. "I won't take on a gladiator without knowing if he can throw a punch, at a bare minimum." If she was going to assume the risk and expense of training him, she had to believe her investment would pay off.

"What do you mean, *you're* going to take on a gladiator?" he demanded.

Velia realized Lucullus may not have explained the situation fully to him, but that could wait. She darted forward and stamped hard on the man's sandaled foot.

He let out a yelp of pain. She aimed a punch at his face, which he dodged. Before she could do anything else, his fist drove into her stomach, forcing all the air from her lungs.

Wheezing, Velia dropped to the ground, curling in on herself as she struggled for breath.

The volunteer stumbled back, raising both hands. "She made me do it!" he protested to Lucullus, who watched the exchange with his usual cool oversight.

The training gladiators around them had paused to stare at them. As she fought to draw air into her lungs, Velia noticed Ferox had risen to his feet from the bench on the edge of the space, his eyes fixed on them.

She lifted a hand. "It's—fine," she croaked. A smile rose to her lips. That punch had been worth it, for it had revealed a very valuable piece of information.

She labored to stand. "You're left-handed," she said to the volunteer.

He stared at her for a moment, then shrugged. "I guess I am."

A left-handed gladiator was extremely useful, as he could more easily get behind his right-handed opponent's defenses.

"What's your name?" she asked.

"Calvus," he replied.

"We'll be changing that." She'd have to think of a suitably impressive name for him. "Here's how this will work. I'll cover your food, lodging, equipment, training, and any medical care you require. If you die, I'll cover your funeral arrangements. I'll keep the fees from your appearances, but any winnings are yours."

He narrowed his eyes, glancing between her and Lucullus. "You're a woman. What do you even know about gladiators?"

"More than you, I'd wager." Velia had never expended much energy worrying about how unconventional it was for a woman to manage gladiators. She knew several women who ran businesses, everything from operating market stalls to running workshops to renting out properties throughout the city. This wasn't much different—only in that her wares would be gladiators.

The volunteer made an unconvinced noise.

Velia lifted her chin. "The next two months are going to contain the biggest games the city has seen in our lifetime. You could be famous by the end of them."

He considered for another moment. "If I die, I want twelve mourners at my funeral."

She pressed her lips together. That would be expensive, but she'd just have to bet on him not dying. "Agreed. So, do we have a deal?"

He nodded. "We have a deal."

A broad smile spread across her face. "Excellent. Let's find you a room."

As she led him toward the barracks, she almost felt as if she could skip with happiness—though she maintained a dignified air in front of her new recruit.

She'd done it. Her first gladiator. Now, if she worked hard to make him a success, the life she wanted would finally be within her reach.

3

VELIA FOUND AN EMPTY room for Calvus—she'd pay her uncle rent for the use of the space—and then sent him off to gather his belongings from wherever he'd previously lived. He hadn't stopped looking at her with that air of suspicious disdain, but he'd managed not to say anything outright disrespectful. They would get to know each other soon enough, she reasoned, and hopefully build the sort of professional rapport that existed between Lucullus and his gladiators.

After her novice left, her mind turned to what came next. He would need training. Velia knew many things about the world of gladiators, but the intricacies of combat and physical fitness were not among them.

She needed a trainer. Perhaps she should have thought of that before acquiring a completely inexperienced gladiator, but there was no time like the present.

Velia stood on the edge of the training ground and surveyed the gladiators. Some stretched, some lifted weights, some swung blunt swords at wooden posts. Others ran laps around the open area or sparred with each other.

Her gaze lit on Jason, seated next to Lea as he wrapped a length of cloth around his knuckles. Jason was talented, experienced, and had a mellow, easy-going attitude. He'd make an excellent trainer for her novice.

She walked over to the two of them. Jason greeted her with a nod. Lea, occupied in tightening the leather armguards she wore, ignored her.

Velia addressed Jason. "How would you like the opportunity to make a little extra money?"

He raised his eyebrows. "Doing what?"

"Training my new gladiator."

His brows lowered. "Sorry, Velia. The next few months are going to get hectic once the games are opened, and I don't want to spend my free time chasing after a novice who barely knows one end of a sword from the other."

"He knows more than that," Velia protested. "Didn't you see him earlier? He can throw a punch." Her stomach was still sore, in fact.

"Punching a defenseless woman does not mean he has any talent for fighting," Jason said.

Velia scowled. "I'm not defenseless."

Jason rolled his eyes. Velia sensed the matter was closed, so she turned to Lea, bestowing a winning smile upon her. "What about you, Lea?"

"No," Lea said shortly.

Velia sidled closer to where Lea sat. "Money aside, I know you'd love the chance to boss around a man."

Lea gave her a sidelong glance. "Not that man. His hair gives me a headache."

Velia knew better than to pester Lea once her refusal was given, so she set aside the matter for the moment and changed the subject. "I also need to think of a good name for him. I was thinking maybe *Achilles*." It was the name of the greatest warrior who'd ever lived, so it would be perfect for Rome's next gladiatorial legend. "And with his hair…Achilles the Fire-Haired. That has a nice ring to it, doesn't it?" She could already imagine hearing that name booming over the crowds in the announcer's deep voice, chanted by an adoring audience as her gladiator claimed another victory…

Jason and Lea exchanged a glance.

"Well, what do you think?" Velia prodded.

"It's a rather ambitious name for a novice," Jason said.

"That's why I thought of it," Velia said. "He's my first gladiator. We have to make an impression." If she was going to do something, she'd jump in with both feet. Not tiptoe or test the waters.

Jason shrugged. "Sounds like you've made your decision."

Achilles the Fire-Haired. Velia smiled. It was perfect.

But the perfect name was worthless if he got himself killed or maimed in his first fight, so she still needed a trainer. She glanced around the ludus, evaluating the other gladiators. She needed someone experienced…

Her gaze lit on Ferox, conducting stretches in a corner of the training area. *Twenty wins out of thirty-two fights.* He might not have Jason's affability, but he was unquestionably the most experienced and successful gladiator she'd ever met, which meant he was just the man for the job.

After less than a day of training, every muscle in Ferox's body ached. He'd become more out of shape than he realized. It didn't help that he'd slept poorly. Hector's ghost was at his most vengeful when Ferox was asleep, tormenting him with a never-ending replay of the moments before Hector's death. In the dream, Ferox ran into the arena, sword in hand, knowing that if he could just get there in time, he could save Hector. But the sand sucked at Ferox's feet, immobilizing him, and he could never make it, instead forced to watch as his friend was slaughtered. The tide of powerless anguish was just as strong as it had been that day.

At least now, in the hot, bright sunshine, he had some distance from last night's nightmares. The ache in his muscles was an excellent distraction, reminding him how hard he'd need to train to get back to where he'd been. His first match was set for the opening day of the games, three weeks from now. The discomfort of sore muscles was vastly preferable to the agony of a wound.

But amid his back's protests as he dropped into a deep forward bend, he wondered if he was too old for all this. Velia's comment earlier had cut deeper than she probably realized or intended. *You're huffing and puffing after one practice match as if you've climbed Mount Olympus.*

He was already thirty, and few gladiators were still fighting at his age, either having retired or died. Maybe he'd been a fool to think he could come back as if no time had passed. Maybe he'd been blinded by Lucullus's money—but it wasn't simple greed that induced him to accept the offer. He didn't want money for its own sake, but for the life it could build him. A hundred thousand sestertii could see him settled in Hispania with a steady income swelling his coffers, far from the ghosts of the arena.

A pair of sandals intruded into his vision, and a throat cleared. Ferox pulled up sharply from the bend, wincing. Velia stood before him once again, her gaze running over him with that unsettling forthrightness.

"What?" he grunted.

She surveyed him for another moment. The fabric sash of her green linen dress was drooping, and she pulled it tighter with a quick jerk of her hand. The adjustment caused the fabric to cling to the curves of her slender figure, and Ferox instinctively turned away to pick up a waterskin lying on the ground nearby.

Though she was very beautiful, he did not waste time desiring women he couldn't have, and his manager's niece definitely fell into that category.

Even so, he was itching to know how she'd ended up here, working for her uncle.

She took a step closer, brushing a curl of fair hair over her shoulder. Locks escaped from her messy braid at every opportunity. "I want to hire you to train my novice."

"*Your* novice?"

Velia nodded as if there were nothing so unusual in that sentence. "My first. First of many, hopefully." She seemed to have no idea that managing a troupe of gladiators was not something aspired to by normal women.

"The man who punched you earlier?" Ferox had witnessed that strange interaction. He'd been recovering on a bench after a set of sprints, but the sight of the red-haired man's fist driving into Velia's unprotected stomach had jolted him to his feet.

"I asked him to fight me. I wanted to see how he moved. And did you notice he's left-handed?"

"Yes." Ferox took a deep drink from the waterskin. A left-handed gladiator was an interesting prospect. Ferox had once tried to teach himself to fight with his left hand, but it was nearly impossible to achieve the same quick, intuitive movements.

"I know you've only been contracted for three fights," Velia said. "Surely you'll need something else to occupy your time. You'll be bored otherwise!"

In Ferox's experience, boredom was a blessing. He said nothing to that; he had a feeling she was the kind of person who didn't require a response in order to keep talking.

He was right. "As for the money," she continued, "I'll offer a portion of the fees from each of his appearances."

"How much?" he couldn't help asking. He didn't want to get entangled with this strange woman and her untrained gladiator, but if money was involved, he'd be a fool not to at least consider it.

"A quarter."

That was far too little. "Half," he replied instantly, then clarified: "Not that I'm agreeing to this."

She narrowed her eyes. "I'm the one taking on all the expenses of his upkeep. I can't split the fees half and half with you."

"You can if you want him to survive more than one match," he shot back.

She considered him for a long moment. Her eyes were a peculiar shade, he noticed, one that shifted between blue and gray, like the sky when it wasn't sure if it wanted to rain or not. "Deal," she finally said.

"Wait—I didn't agree to anything—"

A smile curved her lips, and she cocked her head. "I think you did. Half the fees in exchange for training. You can start tomorrow."

Ferox felt as if the sand was shifting beneath his feet. He couldn't find his footing, thrown off-kilter by this woman's delusions of managing a gladiator.

She turned to leave, but this conversation wasn't finished yet. His hand flashed out, grasping her wrist. Her skin was warm, and her arm seemed as flimsy as the stem of a flower. He felt as if he could break her with a single clench of his fist; he'd broken the bones of men much bigger than her with his bare hands before.

The awareness of her fragility prickled over him like a scratchy cloak, and he dropped her arm.

While Velia might be dainty in appearance, her manner was anything but. In less than a day since meeting her, he'd already witnessed her somehow acquire a gladiator, get punched in the stomach by that same prospective gladiator, and now she seemed bent on trapping Ferox into some sort of agreement to train her novice.

"If we are to…work together…" The words tasted strange in his mouth. "…which I'm still not agreeing to, mind you…then I have some questions."

"Oh? Well, perhaps I have some answers." She grinned as if this was all a grand entertainment.

He started with the question that had been at the forefront of his mind since meeting her. "How does a girl like you end up here?"

"A girl like me?" She gave her head a coquettish tilt, but her eyebrows twitched in a way that hinted at real surprise, as if it had never occurred to her that her presence here might raise questions.

"The only women I've seen within these walls are either slaves, prostitutes, or Penthesilea. You're none of those."

"No," she agreed. "I'll tell you the truth, if you really want to know, but it may scandalize you."

"I'm not easily scandalized."

"We'll see about that," she chuckled. She ambled over to a nearby bench and perched on it. Ferox tried not to notice how the change in position made the fullness of her thighs more prominent against the wooden board. She patted the spot next to her, but he shook his head. He needed to keep some distance between them, as if circling an opponent he wasn't ready to engage yet.

"My parents sent me to live here a year ago," she said. "It was only supposed to be for a month, but, well, I liked it, so I stayed."

"Your *parents* sent you here?" Parents were supposed to protect their children. Especially their daughters. What kind of parents sent their daughter to live somewhere as insalubrious as a gladiator training school, unprotected, surrounded by the roughest of men?

But Velia, from the little he had seen of her, seemed to be thriving in her unconventional home. She fascinated him. He couldn't imagine someone—a young woman, at that—making a *choice* to live here. As opposed to having no better options, like those who volunteered, or having no options at all, like those enslaved as he'd been.

She sighed. "My coming here was a punishment—at least, it was meant to be. Growing up, my parents always threatened to send me to live with my uncle in Rome if I displeased them. They told all sorts of stories about him. I half-expected him to have scales or horns when I first came here." She laughed. "But last year, they finally had enough of me and made good on their threat."

"What in the underworld could you have done to deserve that?"

"That's the scandalous part," she admitted. She glanced down for a moment, the first hint of diffidence she'd shown. "I don't know if you've ever lived on a farm, but it's extremely boring. More than boring—it was suffocating." She tossed her braid over her shoulder. "I needed to *feel* something. To pretend I had some sort of control over my life. So I may have engaged in some…unwise behavior." Her gaze lifted to his, and a hardness entered her blue-gray eyes, as if anticipating his scorn and disgust.

He took a step closer. "What sort of unwise behavior?" He had a fairly good idea from the way she was speaking, but he wanted to hear the truth.

"I think the polite way to put it is that I was rather free with my affections." Her mouth quirked. "The impolite way would be that my mother caught me mid-tumble with a man."

Heat gathered on his face, which irked him. Why was *he* the one who found this embarrassing to discuss? He wasn't sure what to say, but he felt some acknowledgment was needed, so he offered a grunt.

"Do you want to know the worst part? I was atop him so I couldn't even claim I'd been forced," she said with a chuckle.

He recognized that she was attempting to make a joke, but the thought of her atop some unknown man did something strange and thorny to his insides. He gave another grunt, unable to meet her eyes.

"See, you are scandalized," she said with sarcastic triumph.

"Not scandalized," he muttered. "Or if I am, it's at your parents for sending you to live in a place like this. Parents are supposed to protect their children."

He finally dared to look at her, and she cocked her head as if attempting to make sense of his reaction. Her sharp gaze held his. "Well, mine decided I wasn't worthy of their protection some time ago."

Her words made a disorienting feeling rise within him, a strange desire to pull her close and wrap his arms around her and not let go for a very long time. He gave himself a shake to jostle loose the bizarre flood of instinct. *What is wrong with you?*

"So, have you decided you don't want to be in business with a woman like me?" she continued when he didn't reply. "Or are you thinking I'll be free for the taking now that I've confessed my past wantonness to you? I'm not, just so we're clear. I've been chaste as a Vestal Virgin since setting foot in the ludus. Despite being *surrounded* by temptation." She waved an expansive hand at the men training around them.

Ferox couldn't tell if she was joking with that last comment. She must be; if he were a young, pretty woman, the last man he'd want would be a rough, battle-scarred gladiator. But he shook his head. "I wasn't thinking any of that."

"So what were you thinking?" she asked.

4

VELIA WAITED PATIENTLY FOR Ferox to decide what he thought of her. His curiosity about her origins had surprised her. She'd debated concealing the truth or giving him a condensed version of events, but decided she had nothing to hide, not if they were to work together. She wasn't some patrician maiden with a fragile reputation to protect, after all. Now that her parents had given up on her, no one really cared what she did.

Ferox had been oddly shocked at her revelation—not at what she'd done, but at how her parents had retaliated. A strange darkness had swept through his gaze when she spoke of it. She wagered most people would have sided with her parents in this situation. His outrage, though stifled beneath his gruff façade, intrigued her.

Velia didn't like thinking about where she'd come from. Most of the time, she tried as hard as possible to forget everything about the farm, her parents, their disgust with her. But she could still see the revulsion on her father's face, and hear the words her mother spat. *"Stupid whore."*

That was all her parents thought she could be. They'd sent her to Rome to scare some sense into her, thinking it would humble her, turn her into the meek, dutiful daughter they'd always wanted. Instead, she'd discovered a place that filled her with life. Her uncle wasn't the monster they'd portrayed him as; he could be fearsome when crossed, but otherwise he was shrewd, fair, and a master of his trade. The thrill of helping orchestrate the city's most beloved entertainment had quickly ensnared her. There was nothing like the rush of watching one of her uncle's fighters win, hearing the crowd roar their names, and knowing she'd been part of creating such excitement.

Ironically, as she'd told Ferox, she really had been chaste as a Vestal since arriving in Rome. Her life at the ludus provided the excitement she'd been seeking, and she no longer felt that tugging urge toward recklessness that had driven her to tumble a village boy or three in her family's stable. Or hayloft. Or storeroom. Or against a tree in the orchard...

Well, *nearly* as chaste. She was fairly certain Vestals didn't ogle half-naked muscular gladiators as they trained. But ogling was as far as it went.

Ferox was the first one who tempted her to do more than ogle. Perhaps it was just that he was new. Or perhaps it was the wall of gruffness she detected around him. She wanted to dismantle it, brick by brick, to figure out who the real man was. And the best way to tear down all the walls a man tried to build was a good tumbling.

She wasn't supposed to want that anymore. She *hadn't* wanted that since she'd been here. But now, for some reason, all she could think of was how fun it might be to throw her legs over those huge shoulders as he...

"I was thinking," Ferox finally said, pulling her mind back to the question she'd asked him—what he thought of her—"half your gladiator's fees is a fair deal. I agree."

"Excellent." She grinned. "Calvus—I mean, Achilles—has gone to fetch his things. You can start with him first thing tomorrow. I'll get to work on booking his fights."

Excitement leaped within her. In the space of a few hours, she had not only acquired her first gladiator, but had secured the services of one of Rome's most revered fighters to train him. Achilles *had* to be a success under the tutelage of someone like Ferox.

Not bad for a day's work.

The next morning, over breakfast in the vaulted dining hall, Velia brought Achilles over to where Ferox was eating and introduced them.

The men surveyed each other. "Ferox, is it?" Achilles said. "I've heard of you."

"Most people have."

Velia suppressed a grin. A touch of arrogance suited Ferox. He'd earned it, with a career like his.

Achilles turned to her. "I have a complaint," he announced. "There's graffiti in my room. I want it removed."

Velia raised her eyebrows. "There's graffiti in everyone's rooms. Even mine. And Ferox's room has some *very* expressive drawings." She smirked at the memory of what Jason and Lea had inscribed on his wall to welcome him back.

Achilles lifted his chin and gazed down at her with the haughtiness of a patrician. "I want it gone."

Velia crossed her arms. His attitude was annoying, but it wouldn't be too much trouble to paint over it. Maybe doing him this favor would get their working relationship off to a good start. "I suppose I could have someone take care of it."

Ferox rose from the table. "*I'll* take care of it." His voice was low, menace humming behind the words. He picked up a blunt wooden practice sword leaning against the wall and strode toward the exit that led to the barracks.

"You will?" Velia jogged after him, Achilles following.

In the barracks, Ferox reached Achilles's room and kicked the door open. He crossed to the wall featuring the graffiti. It was merely a diminutive penis etched into the plaster, nothing so offensive.

Wielding the sword like an axe, Ferox drove it into the wall. Velia stumbled back a step, and Achilles froze in the doorway to his room. Ferox pummeled the wall again and again, until the graffitied plaster crumbled, revealing the brickwork beneath.

When he finished brutalizing the wall as if it were his mortal enemy, he lowered the sword, breathing hard. "There," he grunted. "It's gone."

Chunks of plaster littered the floor. Velia found herself unable to tear her gaze away from him. A smile slowly spread across her face. He was magnificent. Destructive, yes, but magnificent nonetheless.

That was certainly one way to deal with unwanted graffiti. With the added benefit of terrorizing his new student, for Achilles had turned the color of old milk.

Ferox tossed the sword onto the ground at Achilles's feet, and the novice jumped as if Ferox had lunged for his throat.

"Pick that up," Ferox said, and strode from the room.

Velia spent the rest of the day watching Ferox train Achilles. The incident with the graffiti seemed to have thoroughly intimidated the novice, and Achilles surveyed him with a wary combination of fear and respect.

Ferox was a brusque, unforgiving, and relentless trainer. He pushed the novice hard, so hard Velia began to worry. They began with strength exercises, then Ferox spent some time coaching Achilles on sword maneuvers against a wooden post as an opponent, then moved onto running.

"Are you sure you're not going too fast?" she couldn't help asking at one point. Achilles seemed nearly on the verge of collapse after running laps around the training ground. "It's only the first day. What if he leaves?" Then she'd be back to zero, and she already owed Lucullus money for Achilles's housing and food, even if only for a day. What if she couldn't find another suitable recruit in time for the games?

Ferox cast her a dispassionate glance. "Let him leave. If he flees after one hard day, he was never going to make a success of himself for you. Better for him to know what he's getting himself into from the start."

"If you say so," she replied uncertainly. Achilles had dropped onto a nearby bench, breathing hard, his forehead dripping with sweat.

Ferox's dark gaze lingered on her. "You hired me to train him, Velia. Let me train him."

Hearing her name in his gravelly voice made her stomach quiver and flip. Heat flooded her. If she'd been on her parents' farm and encountered a man who intrigued her as much as Ferox did, she wouldn't have hesitated to use her charms to entice him into a hasty encounter in the hayloft or a secluded corner of the orchard.

Men were so easy to enrapture. All it took was a saucy smile, a suggestive comment, a hand on the chest, and she could take what she wanted from them.

Those days were behind her. She was different now. She had a life that made her happy, a goal for the future that filled her with purpose. She didn't need the thrill of an illicit tumble to distract her from everything she lacked.

Besides, Ferox was the one man she definitely shouldn't take liberties with. Ferox's expertise and training were essential to Achilles's success. If things went badly between them, it could ruin everything.

But there was something about him she couldn't easily ignore. In the past, she didn't really *think* about the boys she desired for longer than it took to figure out if she wanted to tumble them and how she might accomplish that. Ferox, however, had been lurking in her thoughts since she met him.

Her mind was full of questions about him. Why had he left the ludus? Why had it taken such an outlandish offer to get him to return? Was there anything to the way she occasionally caught him glancing toward her as he worked with Achilles? Was it just annoyance at being supervised, or...

Ferox marched forward to haul Achilles to his feet. Though the men were matched in height, Ferox handled the lanky novice as easily as if he were Velia's size. Ferox thrust a blunt sword into his hand and shoved him toward the wooden posts on which gladiators practiced swordplay.

Velia tried not to notice the way Ferox's muscles bulged and rippled, tried not to imagine him handling her in that rough, domineering manner.

Her days of indulging in such pleasures were long past, she decreed regretfully to herself. Ferox was her trainer, not her plaything, and she had to remain focused on her goal.

5

To Velia's relief, Achilles didn't leave. A week of rigorous training passed. Velia thought she could already see new muscles forming on the novice's body. He was learning the basics of combat, though Ferox seemed to be focusing more on general exercises like running and lifting stone weights to build strength. Ferox was a thorough, if relentless, teacher.

Once she was sure Achilles wouldn't abandon her, she met with Oppius, the official in charge of booking gladiators for the upcoming games. The middle-aged man had an office, but Velia knew he would more likely be found at one of three taverns nearby. He wasn't at the first one, but she found him at the second, tucked into a corner with a jug of wine on the table before him. Another man sat at the small table across from him, and Velia recognized him as the manager of another ludus. Oppius must be busy as the games approached, and Velia hoped there would still be space for Achilles in the roster.

Velia lurked off to the side, waiting patiently for the conversation to finish. As soon as the other man vacated his stool, Velia swooped in.

"Velia," Oppius greeted her as he topped up his wine cup. "I thought everything was already settled with Lucullus. I've got all your men on the schedule."

"I have one more for you," she said. "A new recruit. His name is Achilles. Surely there's another novice you can pair him up with. You know how much the crowd loves a fresh face." Matches between novices were always of great interest to the audience; everyone wanted to predict who the next favorite would be and declare they'd supported him from his very first match.

Oppius considered. "I might be able to squeeze him in."

"You're going to want to." Velia leaned forward. "I have three reasons for you. Firstly, his hair is the most blinding shade of red you've ever seen. Hurts your eyes to look at. It's *very* distinctive. People will love it."

Oppius looked unimpressed, so she plowed on with her second reason. "Also, he's left-handed. Quite rare, isn't it? Once he's trained up, that alone will give him an edge over nearly everyone."

Oppius lifted his wine cup to his lips.

"And speaking of training…" Velia allowed her lips to curve into an anticipatory smile. "I've gotten Ferox to train him."

"Really?" Finally, interest sparked in Oppius's gaze, and he set down his cup. "Ferox is training him? I heard Lucullus managed to get him back…"

Velia nodded, feeling absurdly proud of herself. "They've been working from sunup to sundown."

"That is interesting," Oppius murmured. "Can the best gladiator in the city turn an absolute novice into a serviceable fighter in a matter of weeks? Everyone will want to find out."

"Oh, he can," Velia assured. "So, you'll take him?"

Oppius nodded. "I do have a slot or two to fill. I can give you a thousand sestertii for his first appearance. I'll include it with the rest of the fees I owe Lucullus."

"Thank you, but this one will be paid directly to me," Velia said. "Achilles is my gladiator."

Oppius's eyebrows shot up. "*Your* gladiator? Does Lucullus know of this?"

"Of course. He suggested I take Achilles on in the first place."

Oppius leaned back, crossing his arms over his chest. "Are you sure about this, Velia? I know you've been working for your uncle for a while, but there's a difference between taking messages and managing your own gladiators. Listen, you're young, pretty…wouldn't you prefer to find a nice man to settle down with before it's too late?"

Velia tilted her head coyly. "Is that an offer?"

Oppius raised his eyes skyward in exasperation. "Not if my wife has anything to say about it. I only meant, if word gets out that you spend your days managing gladiators, no man is going to want you."

His voice was earnest, and Velia knew he meant well. Oppius was a generally reasonable man, and had barely batted an eye when Velia began showing up as Lucullus's representative. But it seemed his sense of propriety drew the line at her actually managing her own gladiators. "I can live with that."

"I have a nephew," Oppius continued. "Very nice. Not bad-looking. He runs a workshop that makes garum. It's very profitable, you know. I could introduce you."

Velia wrinkled her nose. "Not interested. Especially in someone who probably smells like fish guts all the time." She was done with this line of conversation, and she held out her hand, palm up. "Do you want my novice or not? Remember, he's Ferox's protégé."

Leaning on Ferox's fame was the right move, for Oppius surveyed her for another moment, grumbled something under his breath, and sighed in defeat. "All right. Deal."

She rewarded him with a smile. "Thank you. You won't regret it, I promise. Achilles is going to be the talk of the city by the time the games are over."

Velia walked back to the ludus, bouncing the pouch of coin from Oppius in her hand. Despite her excitement over booking Achilles's first match, a nagging voice in her head questioned if it was too soon. The games were only two weeks away. What if Achilles needed more time to train?

No, it had to be this way. He'd face another novice, so they'd be evenly matched in skill and experience. As in, neither would have much of either. And the sooner Achilles started fighting, the sooner she'd get paid. The two hundred sestertii she'd received today were just a deposit; she'd get the full amount after the match took place. Once he started winning, she could charge more for his appearances.

After returning to the ludus, she divided the coins into two equal halves, then went to find Achilles and Ferox. It was midday, so they were eating lunch in the dining chamber, bowls of steaming lentil stew on the table before them. Lucullus kept a careful eye on his gladiators' diets to ensure maximum nutrition. They rarely ate meat, except at the public banquet the night before the opening of new games, and mostly consumed hearty porridges and bean stews, along with a special drink made of ashes that kept their bones strong.

Velia addressed Achilles. "I've booked you to fight on the opening day."

Achilles's head jerked up, interest sparking in his eyes.

Velia turned to Ferox, laying half the coins on the table beside him. "This is your half of the deposit."

Ferox swept the coins into his large hand and continued eating.

Achilles cleared his throat. "I have a request," he announced.

Velia raised an eyebrow. "Yes?" Ever since the incident with the graffiti, he had refrained from making any requests or complaints.

"I want a woman," he declared. "At least once a week. All the others have them."

She grimaced. "That might cost more than you're worth."

His gaze raked over her in an evaluative manner. "If you're looking to save money, I can make do with you, but I'd prefer one with larger breasts."

A growl rumbled in Ferox's chest. Velia shot him a quelling look as she considered the request. It wasn't such an abnormal ask. Achilles was right; gladiators were usually given regular access to a courtesan. And with his first fight coming up, perhaps it would keep him happy and motivate him to train harder.

"I'll arrange it for the day before the games, as a reward for all the effort you've been putting into training," she finally said, though in fact she had no idea how to actually enact such a thing. She'd figure it out. "With someone else," she clarified. "Not me."

Ferox reached over and snatched the mostly finished bowl from Achilles's hands. "Lunch is over. Go warm up."

Achilles sighed, rose to his feet, and trudged away.

Ferox set down the bowl he'd seized. "You shouldn't let him speak to you like that."

"He said nothing disrespectful," she countered. "He was only suggesting a way to be more economical." Her mind turned to this fresh problem she needed to solve. "I need you to help me find a brothel. Somewhere decent, with reasonable prices. I don't know where to go for such things."

His eyebrows shot up. "What makes you think I know?"

She rolled her eyes. "You're a man, aren't you? Men always know where the brothels are."

He glowered at her. "Ask your uncle."

"I can't do that!" The thought of going to Lucullus with such a question made her skin crawl with embarrassment. Besides, this was *her* problem to solve. She needed to show Lucullus—and everyone else—that she could succeed in this independently. This wouldn't be the first time she'd have to engage a prostitute for one of her gladiators, after all. "I suppose I could go looking for a place on my own. Shouldn't be too hard to find, if I ask around—"

"You can't traipse around the streets asking for directions to a brothel!" he hissed.

"So you'll come with me?"

He narrowed his eyes. Finally, his shoulders slumped. "I *might* know a place," he admitted.

"Excellent!" She bestowed a smile upon him—not that he appreciated it, from the way he was glaring at her. "We can go this afternoon once your training is finished."

6

Ferox couldn't believe he was doing this—escorting Velia to a brothel so she could procure a woman for the irritating novice. In Ferox's opinion, Achilles didn't yet deserve such luxuries, but it was up to Velia.

And there was no way he could let her wander the city looking for a brothel on her own. The streets were dangerous, especially for a small woman like Velia. She'd be an easy target for thieves, and he felt unaccountably anxious with her by his side. He needed to keep her close, needed to make it clear to any enterprising ruffians that she was under his protection.

As they left the ludus, he wrapped a hand around Velia's upper arm and drew her alongside him. Dis, she was tiny. His fingers could encircle her entire upper arm.

"Keep a hand on your coin purse," he warned her. The small bag was tied onto the sash around her waist, but a thief could slice it free all too easily.

She tried to yank her arm out of his hold. "Let go of me!"

"No." He kept his grip secure, but not tight enough to cause pain.

She huffed. "I can look out for myself. I do run errands for my uncle around the city, you know."

"You shouldn't." What was Lucullus thinking, sending his niece off on errands without protection? The city teemed with unsavory types who'd be all too quick to rob her—or worse.

He kept her close to him as they traversed the blocks toward the establishment Ferox knew. He hadn't had the inclination or the funds to seek female company since before he'd left the ludus, but he recalled this place from before. Generally, he only sought a woman the night before a match, finding it the best way to distract from the nerves that plagued him no matter how many matches he fought.

As they walked, her shoulder bumped his chest. A flare of heat settled into his skin at the contact. He wanted to release her, to put some distance between them, but her safety was more important, so he dealt with the disconcerting warmth.

It had been a very long time since he'd touched a woman. He'd forgotten how soft their skin was. Hers felt like silk under his palm. He loosened his grip a touch, afraid he'd unintentionally hurt her. If her arm was this soft, he could only imagine what other parts of her might feel like—

He hastily jerked his mind away from such thoughts, focusing instead on navigating around a treacherous pothole.

They turned down a narrow, crooked street. A woman was selling roasted sausages at the corner, and the savory scent washed over him. After years of a mostly vegetarian diet, meat only made him ill, but it certainly smelled good.

Halfway down the street, they reached a building painted a faded red. Illustrations on the outer wall proclaimed the sort of place this was. Velia craned her head to look at them, but Ferox didn't want to linger on the street. He pulled her through the door.

A woman in her forties sat at a table just inside the door. She rose to her feet when they entered, glancing from Ferox to Velia. He didn't know her; the place must be under new management since the last time he'd visited, which was a blessing. He didn't fancy being recognized.

"We're not taking on any new girls," the woman said to Ferox. "Full house at the moment, you see."

He realized what she'd assumed, and he released Velia quickly. She glared at him, rubbing her arm with an exaggerated grimace.

"That's not why we've come," Velia said, addressing the brothel manager. "I want to hire one of your—your ladies, for my gladiator. For weekly visits to our ludus."

The woman's eyes returned to Ferox. "This gladiator? Wait a moment, I know you. You're Ferox, aren't you?" She moved out from behind the table and approached, a suggestive sway to her hips. "Any girl you want, half price. Just tell everyone *this* is your favorite lupanar."

"Not him," Velia clarified. "A different one."

"Well, the offer stands," the woman said, smiling enticingly at Ferox.

"Not interested," Ferox ground out. Though some men might revel in special treatment like this, he hated it. These people didn't care about him—they only wanted to be able to say that Ferox the gladiator was their best customer.

"Once you see my girls, you'll change your mind," the woman said. "One moment." She gave him a sly smile, then disappeared into the back of the building.

Velia waited beside Ferox for the brothel manager to return. She glanced around the room, curious. She'd never been inside a brothel, though one of her parents' favorite insults to hurl was how she'd inevitably end up at a place like this. *Stupid whore, all you're good for is spreading your legs, might as well earn some coin for it…*

She shook off the memories and examined the space. The front room was small and sparsely furnished. No doubt patrons were not meant to linger here. A narrow hallway, down which the woman had disappeared, must lead to the private rooms.

The walls shone bright with fresh plaster, and the tile floor was swept clean. A few oil lamps flickered in niches along the walls, and the air bore the floral scent of some unknown perfume. All in all, it seemed like a decent establishment.

Ferox must have frequented this place before if he knew of it. Her stomach gave a lurch at the thought of him coming here, negotiating a price, disappearing down that hallway with some strange woman…

Velia cast a sidelong glance at him. He hovered in the doorway as if he couldn't decide if he wanted to make a run for it or not. She could still feel the grasp of his hand on her arm from their journey here. Somehow, he'd managed not to actually cause pain. He must have been very careful to moderate his strength. She remembered all too well the brutal, destructive force with which he'd destroyed Achilles's wall. The incident still made her smile.

She recognized his overbearing actions as protection, and her flimsy protests had quickly died away when she realized she appreciated the warm, solid proximity of his body. A bit of manhandling was well worth it.

Four women, followed by the middle-aged manager, emerged from the corridor. The women arrayed themselves in a line before Velia and Ferox. They were all reasonably pretty, with bodies that appeared well-fed and healthy. That was good; Velia couldn't have Achilles catching some malady from a woman.

They were also all ogling Ferox, batting their eyelashes and offering smiles that seemed to promise all sorts of licentiousness. One of them even allowed the shoulder of her dress to slip down, exposing an expanse of golden skin and the swell of a breast.

Velia narrowed her eyes. She stepped in front of Ferox to shield him from their gazes—not that she was large enough to block much of his body. A sudden possessiveness rose within her, and she put her hands on her hips. *She* could ogle her uncle's gladiators as much as she wanted. These other women? Absolutely not.

The less time they spent here, the better. Velia turned her attention to choosing a woman for Achilles. But how? They all seemed, well, *fine*. Then, she remembered Achilles's stated preference for large breasts.

Velia cleared her throat and pointed at the two slenderest women. "Not them. He's requested, er, bosoms of a certain size." Heat rose to her face. Maybe she shouldn't have insisted Ferox come. This encounter was fast becoming the most embarrassing thing she'd ever had to undertake.

The two slender women shrugged and left, not without final lascivious glances at Ferox.

Velia took a hesitant step toward the two remaining women, trying to discern which of them had the bigger breasts.

"Is this what you want to see, love?" the one on the left said, and slid her arms out of her dress. It fell to her waist, exposing a decently large pair of bosoms.

Ferox made a strangled noise as the other woman did the same.

Velia's face flamed. She was perfectly comfortable with her own body, but this was an entirely different situation. And with Ferox here as well—she wondered if it would be preferable for the ground to open up and swallow her down to the underworld.

But she had a task to complete. She took a deep breath and squared her shoulders. The left woman's breasts were larger, but the right woman's appeared rounder and firmer. Which was superior?

Maybe Ferox could make himself useful for more than just protection. He was a man, after all, and this situation clearly required a man's opinion.

She turned around and found him staring grimly at his feet.

"Ferox," she said. "Tell me which is better. For Achilles, I mean." Both of the women were attractive enough, she supposed, but this wasn't about her own opinion.

His gaze flicked up to her face before resuming its focus on the floor tiles. "No."

"Oh, don't be such a maiden," she snapped. If she could stand to look at a few half-naked women, so could he. She poked him hard in the arm, which felt like jamming her finger into a marble wall. *Ouch.* "Tell me which you like better, and then we can leave."

The promise of leaving must have been sufficient inducement, for he lifted his gaze to the two women for the barest moment.

"That one," he grunted, waving a hand in the vague direction of the woman on the right.

Velia exhaled in relief. She wasn't entirely sure he'd even looked at the woman, but she'd take the excuse to be done with this encounter.

The brothel manager dismissed the two women. While Ferox waited, Velia negotiated a rate for weekly visits to the ludus from the selected woman. It cut into her profits more than she would have liked, but she hoped the investment would be worth it if it kept Achilles happy.

"There'll be an extra fee if he leaves marks on her," the woman warned, and Velia nodded in acceptance. She paid in advance for the first visit, and then she and Ferox were on their way.

Ferox let out a deep sigh once they were on the street, as if he'd been holding his breath the whole time they were in there. "That was humiliating," he muttered.

"For the women?"

"For me." He shot her a loaded glower. "You saw the way they were looking at me."

Velia rolled her eyes. "Please. You were probably the best-looking man they've seen all week. All month, even."

His mouth twisted. "They wouldn't have looked twice at me if I wasn't a famous gladiator."

"Don't be ridiculous," she scoffed.

He gave her an unconvinced grunt.

Was he really so dense he didn't see his own appeal? Clearly, he needed her to enlighten him, so she embarked on a list of all his assets. "Gladiator or no, you'd turn any woman's head. You have a jaw that could cut marble. You've got that dark, brooding look about you that women can't resist. And your shoulders—gods, your shoulders are just the sort of thing a woman could imagine throwing her legs over as she's getting—"

"Velia!" he spluttered, jerking to a halt. Now he really looked scandalized. "You shouldn't say such things."

Velia opened her mouth to issue a nonchalant reply, but someone bumped her shoulder from behind as they passed too close in the narrow street. Instinctively, her hand went to her coin pouch, which held the money left over from the transaction at the brothel.

But the stranger's hand was heading there too, and she felt his fingers close around the leather pouch. Without thinking, she shoved the stranger as hard as she could. "Get off me!"

He didn't relinquish his grip, but before she could do anything further, Ferox's fist smashed into the man's face. The thief dropped like a stone, limp fingers releasing the coin pouch.

Velia stumbled back, heart pounding. The handful of other people on the street stopped and stared.

Moving with the brusque efficiency she now recognized, Ferox seized the back of the unconscious thief's tunic in one hand and hauled him out of the middle of the street, dumping him against the wall of the nearest building. He moved the man as easily as one might drag a stool.

Someone on the street lifted a hand and pointed at him, crying out his name. Murmurs of excitement ran through the onlookers.

"Piss off," Ferox growled. He grabbed Velia by the arm, hustling her into the concealment of a nearby alley, away from interested eyes. No one dared follow them.

"Did he hurt you?" Ferox demanded. His hands moved up and down her arms as if checking for invisible injuries.

Velia shook her head. It had all happened so fast, but the thief had barely touched her before Ferox dispatched him. "Did you kill him?" Her voice trembled, though she strove to steady it.

"No." His hands tightened on her shoulders. "You're sure you're all right?"

She nodded. Her pounding heart had slowed, resuming a more moderate rhythm. Now that the danger was past, she could appreciate the close way he was holding her. His frame filled nearly her entire field of vision, blocking out the dingy, shadowed alley.

His grip loosened, as if he was about to release her, but she wasn't ready to relinquish his touch just yet. "I-I do feel a bit unsteady," she said hastily.

He curled one arm around her waist, drawing her close enough that her breasts brushed his chest. "Are you going to faint?"

"No," she breathed, leaning into his hold. "Just give me a moment." *To enjoy this while it lasts.*

He gazed down at her, his dark eyes still assessing her warily, as if he expected an injury to blossom out of nowhere. "This was my fault." His voice lowered to a reproachful rasp. "I'm sorry, Velia. I was distracted. I should have taken better care with your safety."

"Nothing happened," she murmured. "He didn't harm me. He didn't even take my money."

"He should never have gotten within an arm's length of you," Ferox insisted. "He never should have touched you."

Ferox's protectiveness lit a strange, warm fire within her. Never before had anyone deemed her worthy of being protected. Even her uncle, who respected her and made sure others did the same, treated her strictly as an associate, someone there to do a job.

But Ferox's fierce defensiveness made her feel cherished. It was a heady, unsettling sensation. One she wanted to savor for as long as she could.

She shifted closer to him, and his arm around her waist tightened with the movement. His other arm slid over her back, fingers running up her spine.

"You did nothing wrong." She pitched her voice low, so he had to bow his head closer to hear her.

Close enough that, with a slight rise onto her tiptoes, it was all too easy to stretch up and press her lips to his.

In the back of her mind, she expected him to rear back in surprise, to break the kiss. But he didn't.

Instead, his fingers found her jaw, and he gently tilted her face up to meet his. Her hands latched onto his shoulders, needing the support to stay balanced on her tiptoes. Oh yes, those shoulders were just as magnificent as she'd expected, muscled and warm and unyielding.

Her mouth opened for him, and then they were stumbling backward, until Velia's back hit the wall. She was gloriously pinned between Ferox's heated bulk and the brick building.

His hand delved into her hair, and tingles of awareness erupted over her scalp. He drew her head to the side, his lips blazing a path down her cheek to find the sensitive expanse of her neck. Her eyes fluttered shut, overcome by the sensation. The pull of his mouth sent a hungry throbbing straight to her core. Her hands slid down his chest, and she was rewarded with a catch in his breathing.

She arched her body against his, seeking more, *more*—and found what she was looking for in the stiff press of his arousal. Though the incident with the thief had unsettled her, now she felt true unsteadiness, as if she'd collapse in a molten pool of lust if not for his support.

With what little rational thought remained to her, she evaluated the prospect of allowing him to take her in the alley. Assuming he would go along with something like that—despite his evident ardor, he seemed to have a surprising sense of propriety, as evidenced by his near-refusal to look at the unclothed women at the brothel.

The Velia of a year ago wouldn't have hesitated to ruck up her skirt, fumble his clothing aside, and urge him to sink into her then and there.

But the old Velia acted out of recklessness, out of a desire to escape and distract. She had responsibilities now, as did Ferox. She had to see him every day, and if things went sour between them, he could break their agreement, refuse to train Achilles, and then she'd have to start over.

So despite what the tease of his lips and the grasp of his hands were doing to her, despite the lust raging in every inch of her body, she drew back.

He seemed to sense the change in her posture immediately and did the same. She wished he were a bit less perceptive; she could have enjoyed a few more moments of the delight she found in his arms.

They stared at each other. Velia hadn't noticed that the shoulder of her dress had slipped down until Ferox reached out, gently hooked a finger beneath the fabric, and drew it back into place.

Even that brief contact sent another pang of longing through her, but she ignored it.

"We should get back, I think," Velia finally said, trying not to let her reluctance show in her voice.

He nodded, glancing upward at the sky. "It'll be dusk soon."

They left the dingy alley. Once they were back on the street, Ferox lifted a hand to the level of Velia's upper arm. He hesitated for a moment, then closed his hand around her arm, bringing her near to him once more as they made their way back to the ludus.

Velia couldn't help smiling to herself as they walked, grateful he couldn't see her face. If nothing else, she'd learned something very interesting today: the graffiti in Ferox's bedroom was definitely, utterly, wholly a falsehood.

7

As soon as they stepped within the walls of the ludus, Ferox released Velia. He hadn't wanted to touch her again, not after that dizzying kiss, but it couldn't be helped. He would not take any further risks with her safety. On the walk back, he glowered at anyone who came within an arm's length of them, and everyone gave them a wide berth.

Even the simple clasp of his hand on her arm stirred up vexing, greedy feelings within him, and he let her go with relief once they returned. Velia nodded to him, then disappeared in the direction of her room. She hadn't said a word on their walk back. It was unlike her to go that long without speaking. She must be regretting their kiss, trying to figure out how to warn him off.

She shouldn't have worried. He had no intention of trying to repeat that encounter. She was his manager's niece, which was reason enough to keep her at a distance. Lucullus surely wouldn't want her dallying with his gladiators. And she was also paying him to train her novice. Things were too complicated between them.

It didn't matter that her touch, her kiss, made him feel things he thought impossible. Yes, he had found comfort and pleasure in a woman's embrace before, but only ever the night before a match.

And the heat of those experiences now seemed like a flickering candle compared with the inferno that Velia had lit under his skin.

He retreated to his own room, latching the door behind him. Lust crept over him in a relentless itch. He could still feel her pressed against him, her small hands roving over his chest and shoulders. She was so slight that for a moment he'd worried about hurting her, before the desire burned through him and chased away those fears.

That was yet another reason he should keep his distance—he was sure to accidentally hurt her if they did anything further. Velia was too delicate for the likes of him. She deserved a gentler man: a scholar or an artist or someone like that. Not a gladiator whose only skills were fighting and killing.

But he couldn't yet set aside his desire for her. Arousal simmered within him, flaring insistently as he recalled the softness of her lips, the heady taste of her skin.

He sat on the edge of his narrow bed. It creaked beneath his weight. An image rose in his mind: the story she'd told him of why she'd ended up at the ludus—how she'd been caught atop a man, mid-tumble.

Now, in his imagination, it wasn't some faceless man beneath her. Instead, it was himself, feeling the clasp of her thighs around his hips, the press of his fingers into the flesh of her bottom, the grip and slide of her tight sheath around him.

He closed his eyes and thought of Velia—the way she felt in his arms, the way he imagined she'd feel taking him inside her. His hand found his arousal, and a groan hissed through his teeth at that first potent stroke.

It took only a few tight, quick passes of his hand for the pleasure to rise in a hot, rolling tide. He gritted his teeth, riding out the wave. When it left him, he collapsed backward, slumping against the graffitied wall behind his bed, breathless, his mind scrambled.

As the rapid hammering of his heart slowed, the silence settled over him. This was usually when he felt the presence of Hector's ghost, when the memories of his friend's death became impossible to ignore. But now, they felt more remote. Like a storm cloud that rumbled in the distance, rather than pelting him with rain overhead.

He dared to close his eyes, and all that came to him was Velia. Her saucy smile, the businesslike way she'd managed that mortifying encounter at the brothel, the blast of panic he'd felt when he thought the thief might have harmed her.

No, he shouldn't be thinking of such things. It was just desire, simple lust, between him and Velia. Nothing so strange. Nothing that couldn't be solved with some efficient self-pleasure. Nothing that need trouble him any further.

Velia woke early, her linen bedding tangled around her legs. Blinking the sleep from her eyes, she gazed up at the plastered ceiling. Specters from her dream still loomed in her mind, seducing her with wanton images.

She'd dreamed of herself and Ferox, of what might have happened if she hadn't retreated from their kiss yesterday. Her eyes fluttered shut, unable to resist the pull of her lustful thoughts.

She imagined allowing her hand to wander down his strong, broad chest until it found that stiff, tempting arousal. She would have let her fingers explore, stroking him until he lost any restraint he might have had.

Her breath caught, and she tugged up the fabric of the loose tunic she wore to bed. Her fingers slid between her legs, slipping in the dampness that had already gathered. The muscles of her stomach and legs tensed as she stroked herself, trying to imagine what Ferox's big hands would feel like on her. Nothing like her own delicate touch, surely. Though in that moment at the end of their kiss when he'd fixed the shoulder of her dress, his touch had been surprisingly gentle, feather-light on her skin.

She pictured his hands becoming rough, urgent as he pushed their clothing out of the way. And then she'd hook her leg around his, opening herself to him. He'd sink into her, filling her deep, taking her breath away with the sweet ache of it.

In her bed, her thighs fell open, and she pressed one finger into herself, then another. Her other hand circled at the apex of her sex, driving her pleasure higher and higher.

Her back would press hard against the brick wall, shifting up and down as he took his pleasure. She'd cling to him, relying on his strength to keep her upright. She'd anchor one hand on his shoulder and slide the other down to where their bodies joined, finding her own pleasure just as she was doing now. It would be quick, rough; an alley was not the place for a lingering, tender coupling.

She bit her lip to stifle a moan. Need coiled tight inside her, and her fingers moved faster.

She imagined Ferox's movements becoming rougher, uncontrolled, the way his breath would turn ragged as he got closer. His stoic exterior would finally crack, and he'd groan in her ear as he lost himself inside her.

Her climax burst over her, and her body bowed and shuddered against her thin mattress. She wrang as much pleasure as she could from the release. Then, breathing hard, she relaxed back onto the bed. Sweat dampened her forehead and limbs, and residual sparks of pleasure pulsed in her sex.

Velia opened her eyes, forcing herself back to reality. From outside her room, she could hear the noises of others waking, chatting with each other as they headed to the dining hall. With a reluctant sigh, she heaved herself into a sitting position. Much as she might wish to, she couldn't spend all day in bed, lost to her fantasies. She had a job to do…and a very inconvenient attraction to ignore.

8

ONCE VELIA GATHERED HERSELF, she dressed and left her room. She headed to the dining area where breakfast—barley porridge with honey and dried fruit—was currently being served. A collection of gladiators dotted the space, some seated at the narrow tables, others eating while leaning against the wall. She gave them a quick scan, but Ferox was not among them.

Achilles, however, was—but he wasn't eating. He was glaring at Lea, who sat perched atop a table, her feet resting on the bench beneath it. She dangled the tail of her long, dark braid before Nyx, the ludus's unpleasant cat, who swatted at it from where he sprawled on the table beside her.

Achilles cradled a bloodied hand to his chest. "That cat is a fucking *menace*!" he hissed. "This is the second time he's scratched me!"

Lea twirled the end of her braid in front of Nyx. "Most people only make that mistake once," she said coolly.

When Velia first arrived at the ludus, she'd wondered why Nyx was named after the Greek word for night, as he wasn't a black cat. Soon, she'd learned the name reflected the creature's black as night personality. Lea was the only person the cat tolerated. Anyone else who got too close earned either a hiss or a swat.

Velia had at first thought the cat simply preferred females, but she herself had never been able to get within an arm's length of the beast without incurring his wrath.

Achilles's fair skin reddened. "I'm going to break its fucking neck."

Lea glanced up. "You lay a finger on that cat and you'll soon find you have a few less fingers."

Achilles took a step closer. "Is that a threat?"

A sardonic smile curved Lea's lips. "Oh good, you do understand some things." She hopped down from the table, coming to stand before him. She was of average height for a woman, which made her taller than Velia but shorter than most of the men. Even so, Velia didn't miss the tiny backward step Achilles took at her proximity.

Lea crossed her arms. "Why don't we settle this like gladiators?" She jerked her head toward the door to the training ground. "If I win, you never so much as look at that cat again. If you win, you can do as you like with him. Provided you can catch him, that is."

Velia's stomach tightened with anxiety. "Stop this!" She jogged over and hastily inserted herself between them, half-expecting to be incinerated where she stood based on the way they were glaring at each other.

Lea wouldn't issue such a challenge unless she were fully certain of victory. Though Lea only fought in the arena against other women, Velia had seen her spar often enough against the men that she knew not to underestimate her. Besides, Lea had years of experience and training as a gladiator. Achilles had a week. Velia couldn't afford him being injured in a foolish brawl. It would destroy any hope of victory in his first official match.

She shoved a hand against Achilles's chest, forcing him to take a step back. "Everyone knows not to interfere with Nyx. Now you know that too. And *you*—" Velia spun around, facing Lea. "Surely you have better things to do than pick fights with a novice."

Behind her, Achilles spoke. "I wouldn't have fought a *girl*, anyway."

"You had no problem punching Velia the day you got here," Lea retorted.

"She made me!"

Velia raised a hand. "No one is fighting anyone!"

Jason appeared at Lea's shoulder, and Velia relaxed a bit. Jason had always been one of the more reasonable ones, able to calm arguments and broker peace.

"Let him alone," Jason said quietly to Lea. "Velia is right. There's no honor in besting a novice with barely a week of training."

Lea's hot, dark gaze slid from Velia to Achilles. Finally, she took a step back. "If I discover that so much as one whisker on Nyx has been harmed…"

"No one is going to touch Nyx," Velia insisted.

With one last glare, Lea seemed to accept this, and returned to her perch atop the table. Nyx had been watching the proceedings with his vivid yellow eyes, and he gave Lea's hand a bump with his head, as if to reward her for defending him.

Velia faced Achilles. "Did you hear that? You're to leave the cat alone. Just like the rest of us."

He glowered at her. She hoped he recognized that she'd saved him from certain humiliation and probable injury by putting a stop to this brawl. "Fine," he grunted. A muscle in his jaw pulsed. As he turned away, he muttered something under his breath that Velia could only just make out. "Suppose one sow will defend another."

She tensed. "What did you just—"

Before she could finish the sentence, a hand seized Achilles's throat. Ferox barreled past Velia and shoved the sputtering novice against the nearest column. "Say that again," Ferox demanded, his voice a raspy growl.

He'd come out of nowhere; he must have entered while she'd been occupied with Achilles and Lea.

Achilles's panicked eyes flicked from Ferox to Velia and back again. He wheezed incoherently.

"Ferox! Stop it!" Velia shouted. First Lea, now this. Achilles might not have to worry about losing in the arena if the gladiators of his own ludus got to him first.

Ferox loosened his grasp on Achilles's throat just a little, but didn't release him. "Apologize."

Achilles swallowed hard, his throat bobbing against Ferox's grip. "S-s-sorry," he croaked.

"To them." Ferox jerked his head toward Velia and Lea, still with Nyx on the table.

Achilles's face was nearly as red as his hair. His gaze passed from Velia to Lea, and he choked out another apology. Lea acknowledged it with a roll of her eyes.

Velia didn't want an apology; she wanted Ferox to stop throttling her novice. "Let him go, Ferox," she said through gritted teeth.

Ferox narrowed his eyes at Achilles. "If I ever hear you say something like that again, you'll be sleeping on a pillow filled with pig shit. Understand?"

Achilles nodded. Finally, Ferox released the novice, who sprang away from him, rubbing his throat. Ferox jerked his head toward the door. "Five laps."

"I haven't even eaten breakfast yet!" Achilles protested.

"*Now*," Ferox said. "Or it'll be ten."

Achilles shot them both a glare laden with pique, but turned and trudged toward the door.

Velia exhaled, but she couldn't fully relax just yet. She grabbed Ferox's arm and towed him a short distance from the others so they could speak in private. "You shouldn't have interfered," she snapped.

He looked down at her, his gaze stony and unrepentant. "You can't let him speak to you—or Lea—that way."

"Who said I was going to let him? You didn't give me the chance to handle it." Irritation simmered over her. She'd spent the last year earning the respect of her uncle's gladiators. She knew how to deal with rude comments.

"You made me his trainer," he shot back. "I'm entitled to discipline him for poor behavior."

She folded her arms across her chest. "And I'm his manager. And *your* employer, when it comes to Achilles." She took a small step closer to him, lowering her voice just in case others could hear. "This isn't like yesterday, with the thief. I don't need you to protect me from my own novice."

His eyes darkened at the memory.

"And if you think just because we…because we kissed"—the words tangled themselves in her mouth for a moment—"that entitles you to any claim on defending my honor—"

"No," he snapped. The word was sharp as a knife point. "That's not what I think."

"Good." She gazed at him. This was the first time she'd seen him since yesterday, and the memory of that fiery kiss stole over her…not to mention her fantasies about doing *more* than kissing. A rush of longing stoppered her breath for a moment.

He stepped away from her. "That idiot will short his laps if I don't count them." Without waiting for her to reply, he turned and headed after Achilles.

9

THE DAY AFTER FEROX nearly strangled the man he was supposed to be teaching, he parried the clumsy thrusts of Achilles's wooden sword with rote, mindless movements. The novice wasn't yet skilled enough to occupy more than a portion of Ferox's attention when sparring. Which was unfortunate, given that Ferox could use some distraction. The specter of last night's dream was far too fresh.

In the dream, he'd been standing on the banks of the Styx, icy water lapping at his feet. The sky above was both starless and moonless, a layer of impenetrable black. It didn't feel like being outside on a dark night, but instead had a stifling quality, like heavy fabric.

On the other side of the river, Hector stood, garbed in a black tunic that grew wispy and insubstantial as the hem swirled around his knees. Besides the tunic, he looked as he had when Ferox last saw him. Covered in blood. Skull bashed in. One eye a mangled, gaping hole.

Ferox had always assumed that once a dead man crossed to the underworld, all his wounds would be healed. Seeing Hector like this, wounds as fresh as if they'd just been inflicted, rattled him. Was it possible that Hector would suffer these wounds for eternity?

Two words resounded in Ferox's skull as he gazed at his friend. *Your. Fault.*

Hector wasn't speaking, but the words bore his voice, the lilt of his Germanic accent.

Now, hours later while sparring with Achilles, Ferox could still hear those words. They echoed in his mind like the tolling of a bell. He dealt an extra-hard strike to Achilles's shield, hoping the noise would drown them out. The novice toppled backward and landed on his rear with a curse.

Ferox stepped back, giving Achilles time to pick himself up. Across the training ground, Jason sparred with Lea, chatting amiably. Jason liked to talk as he practiced, and Lea flashed a rare grin in response to something he said.

For a moment, Ferox debated asking them what they thought about Hector and if he might still be suffering in the afterlife. He hadn't let himself mention Hector since his return. Both Lea and Jason seemed to have mourned their friend and moved on, in a way Ferox couldn't. Because it wasn't their fault Hector had died.

With Lea, there was another reason Ferox hesitated to mention their lost friend. Ferox had long suspected that something more than friendship had grown between Hector and Lea, but he'd never dared confirm it. He might be brave enough to face death in the arena, but he was decidedly *not* brave enough to ask Lea about her intimate affairs. Especially after Hector's death.

As for Jason, his grief had taken the most practical shape. Jason had pulled strings to face Hector's killer in the arena and dispatched the man with the swift efficiency their friend had been denied. Ferox wished he'd been the one to exact justice. Maybe that would have soothed his guilt. But at the time, Ferox had still been recovering from the minor injury that led Hector to fight in his place, so Jason was the one to avenge the killing.

Achilles was on his feet again, so Ferox positioned himself for another bout, pausing to correct the novice's starting stance. As they sparred once more, Ferox discarded the notion of mentioning Hector to his friends. This was his burden to carry. Speaking to Lea or Jason about it would only reopen the wound, and this time, he could at least spare his friends that.

In the following weeks, Ferox threw himself into the project of training Achilles. The novice wasn't hopeless. His height and his left-handedness gave him a distinct advantage, and though he loved to complain about the tiniest things that bothered him, like a splinter from the wooden sword or chafing from his greaves, he seemed to take the training seriously.

Ferox intentionally went easy on him; since Achilles would fight another novice who matched his negligible skill level, it was more important to build mental and physical stamina to endure a longer fight than for Ferox to vanquish him in three thrusts of the sword.

They drilled endlessly. Ferox mixed bouts of sparring with exercises that would build strength, like running laps and lifting weights. Teaching refreshed his mind of all the things he'd forgotten in his eighteen months of absence, and the hard training prepared his body as well. He still worried he'd lost too much skill, but he'd soon find out. Both he and Achilles were scheduled to fight on the opening day of the games.

Velia often observed their sessions, likely eager to see how her novice's training was progressing. He could always feel a prickle on his skin when she was watching. It distracted him, but there would be ten times the distractions in the arena itself. He could handle one small woman who made his skin tingle with awareness.

At the end of one long day, two days before the games opened, Velia hung back after Ferox dismissed Achilles. The training area had quieted, most of the gladiators having disappeared to clean up before the evening meal.

Velia glanced in the direction Achilles had gone. "Do you think he's ready?"

Ferox swiped a scratchy cloth over his face and neck, mopping up the sweat that had gathered. "Ready enough not to completely humiliate himself."

She handed him a waterskin. "You should give yourself more credit. You've worked wonders with him. I know he's not the easiest to deal with."

Her praise made a strange, warm feeling rise within him. He took a long swig from the waterskin. "He could be worse. He's like one of those little dogs that yaps and yaps but never bites."

Velia chuckled. "Those little white beasts that patrician ladies carry around? Gods, I'd pay a fortune to pit one of them against Nyx in the arena."

Ferox snorted. "It would be a bloodbath."

She reached out to take the waterskin from him. Their fingers brushed, and suddenly Ferox was back in that dingy alley, his arms full of her slight form, his senses overwhelmed by her closeness.

He jerked his hand back, but she hadn't grasped the water-skin yet, so it fell to the dirt. They both bent at the same time to retrieve it, and their heads smacked together.

"Ouch!" Velia yelped and stumbled back, pressing a hand to her face.

Without thinking, he reached for her. Dis, what if he'd injured her? He'd broken men's noses with his forehead before. His hands closed around her slim shoulders as he anxiously inspected her face for any signs of injury. "Are you all right?"

She blinked up at him, lowering her hand from her face. "Fine." She'd tensed for a moment when he touched her, but now he felt her relax beneath his hands, her muscles growing supple.

He should let her go. He would, right this instant.

But his hands were still on her. He couldn't seem to move them.

She gazed up at him. The fading light caught her blue-gray eyes, glinting like polished steel. Her lips parted, and he felt her body give an almost imperceptible lean closer to his.

Oh no. She was going to kiss him again. Right here in the middle of the ludus, where anyone could see. And he was powerless to stop her. She held him frozen, entranced by the wanting in her eyes, the heat of her body. She was a siren, without need of song to bewitch him.

Heavy footsteps sounded nearby, and finally Velia broke her gaze away from his. He found the will to release her, and she stepped back hurriedly as Achilles trudged toward them, on his way to dinner. He glanced at them with a raised eyebrow, but said nothing. Wordlessly, Velia followed him.

Ferox was relieved at the interruption. After all, the last thing he should be doing was kissing his manager's niece in the middle of the ludus.

Yes, this ache that spread over him at her absence was definitely relief. Not longing, not hunger. Just relief, he told himself as he headed to the barracks.

The next day passed in a blur of final preparations for the opening of the games. Velia was kept busy seeing to last-minute repairs to armor, collecting outstanding fees for tomorrow's matches, and other tasks for her uncle. She relished the activity, as it gave her little time to worry about Achilles's first fight.

Finally, the business of the day was done. As dusk set in, she joined the rest of the ludus for the customary banquet held the night before the games opened.

The banquet took place outside in a public square, with tables and couches arranged beneath a red awning. Torchlight flickered on glassware and silver, and the noise of conversation, laughter, and the occasional drinking song resounded against the walls of the nearby buildings. This way, eager watchers could get an early look at the gladiators as they glutted themselves on food and drink. For once, their restrictive diet was lifted, and meat, fish, and poultry were in never-ending supply.

In a break between courses, Velia rose from the couch beside her uncle and meandered around the perimeter of the space, stretching her legs. Her gaze lit on Achilles, his plate piled high with sausages, duck legs, oysters, and other delicacies.

She slid into the empty spot next to him. "You're going to make yourself ill."

Swiftly, she removed about half the food from his plate and dumped it onto the plate of his neighbor, who was deep in conversation with someone on his other side and didn't notice.

"Hey!" Achilles protested.

"You'll thank me when you're not sleeping in the privy." She didn't begrudge the fighters their indulgences, but she wouldn't take any chances with Achilles's health tomorrow.

He glowered at her and pulled his plate closer, curling a defensive hand around it to ward off further incursions.

She distracted him from his irritation with a question. "The, er, woman I found for you. Was she all right?" The courtesan's first visit had been yesterday, a reward for the effort Achilles had put into his training.

"She had all the necessary parts."

Velia grimaced. "Keep talking that way and you'll have girls lining up from here to the Palatine to fall into your bed."

He rolled his eyes, then sank his teeth into the one duck leg remaining on his plate.

Velia was already tiring of talking to him, so she rose and sought a more pleasant dinner companion. There was room next to Ferox, and she didn't hesitate to slide onto the couch beside him, tucking her feet beneath her. He wore a light blue toga for the occasion, and while he did look quite dignified, she preferred the sweaty, bare-chested version she'd become accustomed to seeing as he trained with Achilles.

Ferox's plate was filled with only a moderate array of crispy chickpeas, flatbread, cheese-stuffed olives, and skewers of roasted vegetables. She raised an eyebrow. "You're not having any of the meat?"

He shrugged. "Doesn't agree with me."

She grabbed his wine cup and looked inside. The wine was blush pink, well-watered. "You're hardly drinking, either."

Another shrug. "I don't want a headache tomorrow morning."

She stretched out on the couch next to him. She wasn't used to dining on couches, and lying next to him like this felt oddly intimate—as if they were in bed together, not at a banquet.

In her experience, even the most seasoned gladiators strove to distract themselves the night before a match, and that distraction usually fell into three categories: food, wine, or women. Often all three. But Ferox wasn't glutting himself on food or wine.

So that left women.

"You're going to visit a brothel," she realized aloud. Her stomach lurched. It would probably be the place they'd visited together; the manager had offered him half-price on any girl, after all. He'd be a fool not to take advantage of such a bargain. But the thought of him with any of those women…

He popped an olive into his mouth, chewing and swallowing before speaking. "Maybe," he said evenly, shooting her a cool sidelong glance. "Why shouldn't I?"

"Because…" That question required some consideration. To buy time, she reached out to help herself to a handful of chickpeas from his plate.

He looked askance at her pilfering but made no comment.

Because the thought of you with someone else makes me want to break something. Because I've wondered what it would be like to lie with you since the moment I met you. Because I haven't wanted anyone like this…ever?

"Because it would be a waste of money," she finally said.

He blinked at her. Leaning on one powerful arm, he pushed himself into a sitting position. "What do you—" He broke off to clear his throat, as if it had suddenly gone dry. "What do you mean?"

"Come back to the ludus with me," she murmured, lowering her voice so none of their neighbors would hear. "Don't waste your coin on a brothel."

She didn't care how brazen she sounded. He might die tomorrow. It was doubtful, but possible. And she couldn't let him possibly die without taking him to bed.

All the reasons she'd ended their kiss now seemed meaningless. Perhaps it was still dangerous to muddle her relationship with the man she'd hired to shape Achilles into a successful gladiator, but none of that mattered when Ferox was about to face death in the arena tomorrow.

The rapidly shrinking rational part of her brain reminded her he was extremely unlikely to die, based both on his skill and the fact that he was beloved by the people.

But that rational part of her mind was easy to bury beneath the simple fact that she wanted him. And this time, wanting him wasn't about defying her parents or chasing a thrill. It was about *him*—how she felt when he touched her, the way his presence drew her to linger near him whenever she could. How many hours had she wasted watching him train Achilles when she could have been busying herself with errands for her uncle?

Ferox met her gaze. The shock faded from his dark eyes, laying bare a hunger that echoed the growing ache of need in her core.

Silently, he rose from the couch and helped her to her feet. Velia anticipated the others were too occupied with their feasting and carousing to notice the two of them leaving together, but if someone spotted them, she hardly cared. She had no reputation to protect, and she was no longer beholden to anyone's ideas about how she should conduct herself.

Without a backward glance, she left the banquet behind, and walked with Ferox to the ludus.

10

APART FROM A SURLY guard at the entrance, peeved at missing the festivities, the ludus was empty. In the barracks building, shadows cloaked them as Ferox led Velia to the door of his tiny room. The whole walk back, he'd been waiting for her to change her mind. Perhaps now she'd come up with some excuse, some reason to disappear.

But as soon as he opened the door, she walked straight in, as bold as if it were her own room. A smirk lifted the corner of her mouth as she beheld the graffiti that still adorned his wall.

Ferox turned away to light an oil lamp, which rested on a shelf bolted to the wall. It filled the room with a warm, flickering glow. He paused for a moment, his back still to her. How should he go about this? He hadn't lain with a woman since the night before his last fight, over eighteen months ago. His prior partners had all valued efficiency when it came to bedding; the faster it was over, the faster they could move onto their next customer.

But with Velia, he wanted to take his time.

When he turned back around, Velia was standing in the middle of his room, gazing steadily at him. He envied her composure. Being alone with her, his stomach was a riot of nerves—a welcome relief from worrying about tomorrow's fight.

At the banquet, she hadn't been entirely correct in assessing his plans for that evening. He hadn't yet decided whether he was going to seek out a woman. After so long away from the arena, he felt as tense and ill-equipped as he had before his very first fight, and a night with a woman was the most reliable way he'd found to distract himself.

But he'd spent most of the banquet surreptitiously eying Velia from across the table, and he came to the uncomfortable realization that he didn't want a quick tumble with a woman whose name he'd never remember, a woman who was only bedding him because he paid her to.

He wanted Velia. And somehow, she was in his room—real and warm and so, so beautiful.

Velia was bold enough that he half-expected her to take charge of the situation. To his surprise, however, she did nothing, only stood there watching him. Waiting.

He recognized her inaction not as hesitance or uncertainty, but as something else. She, after all, had initiated their kiss and had been daring enough to flat-out proposition him in the middle of the banquet.

Now, it was his turn to prove how much he wanted her.

He approached her. She tilted her face up, holding his gaze. His arms slid around her, and the pleasure of holding her stole his breath for a moment. He lowered his head and kissed her. She let out a sigh against his mouth and pressed closer. Arousal flared, quickening his heartbeat.

His palms tingled with the desire to feel her bare skin against them, and he didn't deny himself. He found the fabric sash at her waist and untied it. Then, his hands went to the shoulders of her dress, pulling them down. The loose dress gave way easily, baring her breasts and then falling to the floor in a heap of fabric.

His breath stuttered in his throat as he beheld her. He forgot how to breathe, to move, to think. The low light didn't do her justice; she deserved the blaze of high noon sunlight to bathe every inch of her perfect body.

But since the sight of her shadowed body was nearly enough to undo him, perhaps it was for the best they didn't have more light.

Her body was slight but womanly, with a swell of breasts and hips usually kept well-hidden beneath her clothing. She was formed with a fineness that reminded him of figures on painted vases—so exquisite she couldn't possibly be real.

He reached for her, taking her into his arms again. Her small breasts were just enough to fill his palms, and she shivered as he gave them a gentle squeeze.

"How do these compare to those women at the brothel?" she asked.

"What women?" he replied dazedly, much too occupied in skimming his thumbs across her hard nipples to comprehend her words.

She gave an unsteady chuckle. "Good answer."

He lowered his head to take one of her nipples into his mouth. She let out a sharp gasp and arched against him. Her hand slipped between them, and when it found his cock, he broke off from his enjoyment of her breasts with a ragged groan. Even through the layers of fabric separating them, her touch made him stiffen and ache.

But he needed more, needed to feel her on his bare skin. He struggled out of his clothes. In an attempt to look respectable for the banquet, he'd worn a toga, which he hated. He found the garment heavy and restrictive, and always feared that with one wrong move the carefully arranged folds would collapse in a pile of tangled fabric.

Hands clumsy with urgency, he somehow extricated himself from the miles of wool, balling up and tossing the fabric into the corner of the room. Then, he stripped off his short-sleeved tunic.

Finally, he was bare to her gaze. Her eyes roved over him. He knew he didn't look like a perfect specimen of a man; his skin was scarred in many places from various fights over the years, most of which he didn't even remember. But there was no mistaking the appreciation in Velia's eyes.

Her hands soon followed her gaze, making straight for his cock. Her slender fingers wrapped around him. Desire surged at her touch, and he strove to master himself.

"I knew that graffiti was a filthy lie," she said with a grin, her eyes sliding to the defaced wall. "Under-promise and over-deliver, indeed."

He wasn't capable of summoning a suitably clever reply, so instead he walked her backward, until her calves bumped the edge of his bed. He put a hand on her shoulder, meaning to lay her down, but she stopped him with a raised hand.

"One thing first." A note of breathlessness entered her voice, which pleased him: a small sign she was as affected as he was. "I don't wish to risk a child. There are herbs I can take, but it's safest if you withdraw."

He nodded. "I understand." He should have thought of that sooner, but his mind had been too scrambled by the thrill of having her in his room, naked.

With that settled, he gently but firmly pressed down on her shoulders.

She let out a pleased giggle and yielded easily, lowering herself to sit on the bed. She moved to shift backward, but Ferox caught hold of her knee, keeping her in place with her legs draped over the edge of the bed, feet on the floor.

He sank to his knees between her legs. He trailed his fingers down the insides of her thighs, touching her as lightly as he was capable of. Her skin felt as soft as the petals of a flower.

He widened her thighs, head lowering toward that tempting place at their summit. The unsteady illumination was not sufficient to fully appreciate her, but he could see the peaks and valleys of her center. A flicker of light caught on dampness gathered at her entrance, and the sight of it made his cock give a painful twitch.

He slid his hands beneath her round bottom and tugged her toward the edge of the bed, angling her hips up toward him.

"Ferox," she breathed. Her hand grazed the back of his head. "What are you—oh!"

His mouth found her, tongue sliding over her sex. The banquet earlier might as well have been ash for how it compared to the taste of her.

Her hand tightened in his hair, and she let out a moan as he explored her with his lips. "No one—no one's ever done this to me before," she gasped.

He managed to tear his mouth away from her for long enough to speak. "So this wasn't what you were imagining when you made that comment about my shoulders?" *Your shoulders are just the sort of thing a woman could imagine throwing her legs over as she's getting*—she'd said on their return from the brothel before he'd cut her off, scandalized.

She managed a breathless laugh. "If you must know, I was imagining getting fucked with my legs over your shoulders."

That image sent an aching pulse of need through him, but he held onto his composure. There would be time for all that soon enough. He hadn't yet had enough of her taste, so he sought her once more with his mouth. His lips closed around the swollen bud at her apex, tugging at it gently. She made a high-pitched noise, so he did it again.

Though he appreciated her experience, there was a deep, primal satisfaction in knowing he was the first to please her in this way. Many would claim that this act was unmanly, degrading to perform.

But Ferox would dare anyone to say that to his face.

Her thighs closed around his head, reducing his entire existence to the feel of her against his tongue, her intoxicating scent, the salty tang of her desire.

Suddenly, he didn't just want to be the first to do this to her. He wanted to be the last. The possessive urge overwhelmed him for a moment. His fingers tightened where he gripped her thighs, pulling her closer. *Mine.*

But just for tonight. Velia was only doing this because of his fight tomorrow—because, for some reason he still couldn't decipher, she objected to the idea of him visiting a brothel. This would be a onetime pleasure, so he'd better savor it.

He continued working her with his tongue, searching for what she liked best. She was responsive and uninhibited with her reactions, not hesitating to move his head where she wanted it.

His cock throbbed, an insistent, demanding pulse between his legs. He ached to wrap his fist around himself, but feared his desire would get the better of him.

So he found another use for his hand. He circled a finger at her entrance. She was now thoroughly soaked, and his finger slipped inside without resistance. Dis, she was tight. She might not be a maiden, but he'd still need to go slowly so as not to hurt her.

"Can you take another?" he murmured.

"Yes," she breathed, so he worked a second finger inside her, feeling her muscles stretch as she welcomed him. She let out a sigh as he filled her.

He experimented for a few moments, finding a rhythm she seemed to like. Then, he bent his head and took her into his mouth once more. Her back arched, and she moaned. The sound sent a cascade of fire through him. She writhed beneath him, and he kept his free hand curled around her thigh, holding her in place.

Her legs clasped tighter and tighter around his head. "Don't stop," she gasped. "Just like that."

With his fingers inside her, he could feel the moment her climax overtook her. She clenched and spasmed around him, hips bucking. Cries burst from her mouth, and Ferox couldn't hold back a groan of his own, muffled against her flesh.

Her hand loosened from his hair, and she collapsed back onto the bed. Gently, Ferox withdrew his fingers, feeling a few aftershocks quiver through her as he did so.

When he raised his head, she gazed up at him, flushed and languid. But there was still wanting in her eyes, and she parted her legs with an inviting smile. Desire pulsed hot and urgent through him, and his restraint was approaching its end.

He slid his hands beneath her hips and moved her into the middle of the bed. She let out a soft giggle as he covered her body with his own. She felt so small beneath him, but she still consumed his entire focus.

"Are you ready?" he murmured, his voice hoarse with need.

She pressed a kiss to his shoulder. "You saw to that quite well."

He took hold of her leg behind the knee and pressed it back, opening her to him. Her leg hooked over his shoulder. "Is this what you imagined?"

"Yes," she whispered.

He reached down to align their bodies. She was soaked and warm and still tight, despite his earlier ministrations, and he lowered his forehead to the mattress with a groan as he eased into her. She wasn't fragile, he knew, but he still needed to take care with her. He could hurt her without realizing it. And he'd need to proceed with caution to make sure he could withdraw at the right moment.

Her hands grasped his shoulders, and her other leg wrapped around his hips as he slowly filled her.

Finally, he found a deep seat inside her. Her hot, tight warmth surrounded him, and when she adjusted her position beneath him, her muscles clenched in a way that made him gasp.

"Good?" he grunted when he was capable of speech.

"So good," she breathed.

Her words gave him leave to move inside her, to thrust. He still went slowly, testing his control, but soon found an angle and rhythm that made her cry out with every thrust. He loved the way she clung to him as he took her. Her arms were wrapped tight over his back, one leg braced against his shoulder while her other leg clasped around his waist as if trying to draw him impossibly deeper.

The narrow bed rattled and shuddered. He didn't care if it collapsed beneath them. For now, all he could think of was her.

The pleasure mounted quickly—too quickly. He'd need to change strategies if this was to last much longer. Ferox withdrew with a hiss and flipped her onto her stomach. She let out a surprised squeak as he took hold of her hips and sank back into her with a groan.

After one sweet thrust, he realized he'd grievously miscalculated in thinking he could last any longer like this. The change in position offered a new angle and an even deeper seat inside her, eroding what little control he had left. He might not be able to see the ecstasy on her face or her pert breasts bouncing with every thrust, but he could still hear her moans, albeit muffled into the bedding. He could see the elegant line of her spine, curving toward him, could feel his fingers pressed into the firm flesh of her bottom…

She arched her back, pulling him in deeper, and he let out a strangled gasp. He tightened his hold on her hips. "Don't. Move."

In the back of his mind, he sensed he was gripping her too tightly, but his capacity for gentleness was dissolving like honey in hot wine.

She gave a throaty chuckle, which broke off into a moan as he thrust into her again. He managed one more, then another, and then the pleasure was swelling, about to burst. He tore himself out of her, hand clasped tight around his cock as he spilled onto her back. The pleasure ripped through him, stealing his breath for several blissful moments.

When it subsided, he collapsed half on top of her, breathing hard. He forced himself to rise, so he wouldn't crush her, and fetched a cloth to clean them both.

She turned her head over her shoulder as he wiped his seed from her back. "Thank you," she murmured.

Ferox tossed the cloth away and returned to the bed. It was barely big enough for him, let alone another person—even one as small as Velia—but she snuggled close to him. He slid his arm beneath her head to pillow it. Even if the bed were triple its size, he'd still want her close.

He'd never spent the night with a woman before, but he found he liked having someone to hold, someone whose breathing could anchor his own.

These were the moments when Hector's ghost usually loomed, the quiet moments before sleep when there was nothing to shield his mind. But tonight, he felt nothing.

As Velia's breathing slowed, so did his, and sleep soon took him.

11

WHEN VELIA WOKE, SHE stared up at the plaster ceiling, confused. It seemed familiar, yet…the pattern of cracks spiderwebbing the ceiling wasn't the one she'd memorized.

She sat up slowly. Her gaze caught on the lurid graffiti decorating the wall next to the bed.

The events of last night came back to her in a rush of wanton images and sensations. She was in Ferox's room. A grin spread across her face as she recalled the pleasure they'd shared.

And today…today was the opening day of the games. Today, both Ferox and Achilles would fight.

Her smile evaporated. Nerves fluttered in her stomach.

She was alone; Ferox must have risen earlier to get ready. She wished he'd woken her before he left.

Velia swung her legs out of bed and rose to her feet—only to stiffen with a cry as a collection of aches and pains made themselves known.

Everything below the waist hurt in one way or another. The muscles along the insides of her thighs ached. Her hips felt strained, overly stretched. And between her legs…those muscles had been exerted in a way she'd clearly become unaccustomed to after her period of abstinence.

She took a tottering step, wincing. She'd noticed no pain or discomfort last night. Indeed, her tumble with Ferox had been the best she'd ever had by a wide margin. But today, her body felt as if it had been run over by a chariot.

She clothed herself, then hobbled to her own room, where she changed into a fresh dress. As she did, her eye caught shadows of bruises along her hips. She sensed they'd perfectly match the span of Ferox's hands.

Velia ran a finger over the marks. She rather liked them. She wasn't the sort to tolerate being bruised by a man, but these marks had been doled out in passion, not violence, and she hadn't even noticed at the time.

Once clothed, she combed her hair, braided it, then emerged into the outdoor area of the ludus, still walking gingerly.

It was nearly empty. A few men lingered in the shade on the other side of the training ground. Closer to Velia, Penthesilea sat in the sun, mending a rip in one of her tunics.

Lea glanced up when Velia approached.

"Has Ferox gone to the arena already? And Achilles?" Velia added hurriedly. Her novice, about to face his first fight, should be her primary concern today. Not Ferox.

Lea nodded. Her sharp brown eyes scanned Velia from head to toe, and a half-smile curved the corner of her mouth. "I didn't think he had it in him," she muttered, as if to herself.

"Excuse me?"

Lea arched an eyebrow. "You spent the night with Ferox last night."

"I—I—" Heat rose to Velia's face. "How did you know?"

Lea rolled her eyes. "If I hadn't seen you two leaving the banquet together, the way you're walking this morning would have told me everything I needed to know."

Velia endeavored to stand up straighter. "What do you mean, the way I'm walking?"

"You're waddling like a goose." Lea snickered. "A goose that's been thoroughly fucked."

Velia glared at her, willing a witty retort to spring to mind. Her brain, however, deserted her. "I have to get to the arena."

"Yes, you should get going," Lea said. "At the rate you can walk, you'll be lucky to get there by sunset."

"Mind your own fucking business," Velia rejoined, but the words had no heat to them. She and Ferox had, after all, left the banquet together in plain view of everyone. She shouldn't have been surprised it caught Lea's attention.

Velia set her jaw and shuffled out of the ludus. Thankfully, the arena was only a block from here, so she didn't have far to walk. Worries about what the day might hold soon distracted her from her aches.

Was Achilles ready? Ferox had made a great deal of progress with him, but still, it had only been a few weeks. What if Achilles sustained an injury that put him out of action for months, costing her money for food, lodging, and medical treatment in the meantime?

She exhaled and sent up a fervent prayer to Fortuna, goddess of luck, to watch over Achilles.

And Ferox too, though she sensed he was skilled enough not to need luck.

After arriving at the arena, she found the back entrance and nodded to the guard, who recognized her and granted admittance to the area where the day's fighters prepared.

Velia wove between people as she searched out her uncle's men. Achilles's flame-red hair caught her attention first, and she went over to him. She scanned the others nearby, but didn't see Ferox yet.

Achilles looked like a true gladiator. He was bare-chested, his lower legs covered with leather greaves. An arm guard made of overlapping metal plates equipped his left arm from shoulder to wrist. His visored helmet rested on the ground next to him, along with a rectangular wooden shield.

He acknowledged her with a nod when she approached, then continued fiddling with a buckle on his arm guard.

"Feeling good?" she asked. Nerves tumbled in her own stomach. She couldn't imagine how he must be feeling.

He gave a short nod.

"Is Ferox here?"

Achilles waved a hand vaguely. "Somewhere."

In his curt answers, Velia recognized he was nervous. Part of her wished Ferox was here to help steady him, but Ferox had his own fight to prepare for. She didn't begrudge him some time to himself. Besides, he'd already done his part in training Achilles.

Velia tentatively laid a hand on Achilles's bare right shoulder. "You'll do well," she said, imbuing her voice with all the confidence she didn't feel. At this moment, all she could remember were the many times she'd witnessed Achilles stumble or drop his shield or miscalculate a strike and fall over.

He shrugged out from beneath her hand and leaned down to pick up his shield, testing his grip on the metal handle.

Please don't die, Velia prayed inwardly.

The waiting was the worst part. Over the next hour, the noise from the stands steadily increased as more and more people filled them. They'd be packed today, on the first day of the games. Loud cheers resounded at one point, signaling the arrival of the emperor and his entourage.

There were several matches before Achilles was up, but each match lasted no more than a quarter of an hour. Soon, it was time. Velia helped him settle the visored helmet on his head and gave him one last awkward pat on the shoulder as they walked to the arena's entrance, a narrow opening between the towering stands. Here, the noise of the crowd was a constant roar, reverberating like thunder.

Lucullus was there, watching the matches from the shadows. He greeted them with a nod.

There was a momentary, partial hush as the announcer of the games intoned an introduction to the next match. Only those closest on the lowermost levels would be able to hear. The words were a blur in Velia's ears, both due to the distance and the anxiety coiling through her.

She struggled to think of something else to say, something suitably encouraging to send Achilles off—but he'd already stepped out into the sandy arena. His first steps were hesitant. His helmeted head craned up at the people crowding the stands. Then, as the crowd cheered in anticipation, his shoulders straightened, his stride lengthened, and he headed for the center of the arena.

The other gladiator entered from the arena's opposite side. An official met them in the center, carefully marking out their starting positions. This man would make sure the match was fought fairly and had the power to declare a draw or call a temporary pause if needed.

As the gladiators moved into position, Velia's gaze swept around the stands. To her right, on the lowest level directly between the two entrances, flashes of red and silver caught her eye: the scarlet-crested helmets of the Praetorian Guard, the emperor's personal bodyguard. She squinted. In the front row, she spotted a man in a rich purple toga. He appeared to be only a few years older than herself, perhaps in his mid-twenties.

"Is that him?" Velia asked her uncle, pointing. "The new emperor?"

Lucullus followed her gaze and nodded. "What a sight," he murmured. "It's been over twenty years since an emperor has presided over the games."

Velia knew the previous emperor, Tiberius, despised the spectacle of gladiatorial combat and had never attended the games, even before he'd become a recluse at his Capri villa in the decade before his death.

Good riddance, in her opinion. The games were as Roman as the toga. How could someone claim to rule Rome and not like the games?

Luckily, this new emperor, Gaius Caesar, didn't share his great-uncle's disapproval. Velia never imagined that she would even lay eyes on an emperor, let alone have him watch her very own gladiator compete. A heady mixture of excitement and pride lit in her stomach. If only her parents could see her now. Well…they probably still wouldn't approve of her, but they'd have to admit it was an impressive sight.

She sent up another desperate prayer that Achilles would not embarrass himself before the most powerful man in the world.

Beside where the emperor sat, six white-garbed women occupied a second private area. Those were the Vestal Virgins, the priestesses who held powers that rivaled the emperor's. They were sworn to thirty years of service, and if they forsook their vows of chastity, the walls of the city would crumble and Rome would fall. The offending Vestal would be buried alive.

Velia didn't envy them. Thirty years of chastity on pain of death was much too high a price even for their unparalleled prestige.

"You've done well with him," Lucullus said, gesturing toward Achilles.

Her uncle's praise warmed her, but she couldn't accept it. "Ferox is due most of the credit."

"But you chose Ferox to train him."

She refrained from mentioning that Ferox had been her third choice, after Jason and Penthesilea. "Ferox has done very well with him."

"You should consider acquiring a second gladiator soon," Lucullus advised. "Take advantage of Ferox's expertise while he's here. I expect that as soon as the games are over, he won't stay a moment longer than he has to."

A strange pang went through her. But of course Ferox would leave once his contracted three fights were finished. Her uncle had said it took an obscenely lavish offer to tempt Ferox to return. Besides, he was already old for a gladiator, and he couldn't fight forever.

At least the games would stretch for two whole months. She didn't have to worry about saying goodbye just yet.

Soft footsteps sounded in the dirt behind her, and she turned to see Ferox, as if her thoughts had summoned him.

Dis, he looked spectacular. His chest was bare, the powerful muscles exposed to the sunlight, thatched with an array of scars. A loincloth, secured at his waist with a heavy leather belt, regretfully hid his most impressive assets. Like Achilles, his sword arm was covered with a plate guard. Outfitted like this, his shoulders seemed broader than ever, and her cheeks heated as she remembered putting them to excellent use last night. No doubt that had something to do with why her lower body felt thoroughly destroyed this morning.

Now, with anxiety over the upcoming fight gripping her, all she wanted was to sink into his arms and bask in the comfort of his embrace. But with her uncle watching, she had to show a bit more decorum, so she greeted Ferox with a polite nod.

"It's about to start." She gestured toward the arena, her chest tight. "I hope he doesn't die."

Ferox stood just behind her, close enough that she could hear the steady rhythm of his breathing. "He won't die. No one dies in their first fight. His opponent isn't skilled enough to kill him, and the crowd doesn't care enough to call for his death."

Velia exhaled, trying to take comfort in his words. "Are you ready for your own match?"

Out of the corner of her eye, she saw him nod. "I had a very restorative night of…sleep."

Velia pressed her lips together against a smile. Luckily, her uncle was staring out into the arena, so he wouldn't notice the flush that was surely staining her cheeks.

The fight began, and Velia forgot all about Ferox's expansive shoulders and warm skin and rippling muscles. Achilles and the other gladiator circled each other. When experienced gladiators fought, this initial circling always had an air of evaluation, assessment; they were noticing each other's height and reach and stride, crafting a strategy for the imminent battle.

But here, the two novices simply seemed to hesitate. Their steps were tentative, as if neither wanted to move too far or too quickly in case it prompted the other to strike.

Boos rang out from the crowd. The official, standing at the edge of the arena, shouted something at the fighters, exhorting them to get started.

Velia held her breath. The other gladiator struck first. Achilles blocked the strike with his shield but stumbled back a step under the force of the blow.

Velia tensed. She edged backwards until she could just feel Ferox's warmth behind her, without touching him. She half-expected him to adjust his position to put more space between them, but he remained where he was.

As the fight progressed, she clasped her fingers together, pressing her entwined hands to her mouth. Achilles's left-handedness allowed him to get a successful thrust behind his opponent's shield. The other fighter had to awkwardly maneuver his shield to defend from the unexpected angle, and Achilles managed to deal him a shallow cut on his chest.

But the wound, rather than weakening the opponent, seemed to spur him to greater energy. Achilles soon found himself on the defensive, stumbling backward, blocking with his shield, unable to launch an attack.

Achilles tripped over an uneven patch of sand behind him and fell flat on his back. He struggled to rise but couldn't find purchase on the shifting sand. He dropped his shield and raised a finger in the signal for surrender. His opponent paused, standing over him with his sword held in an uncertain grip.

Velia's breath hissed through her teeth. She stuffed her fingers into her mouth, chewing anxiously on her nails. Along with everyone else, her attention shot to the place where the emperor and his retinue sat. As the host of the games, he would ultimately decide the fate of each losing gladiator.

Behind her, Ferox stood as calm as ever, his breathing steady. Was he even paying attention? Did he realize Achilles was one man's whim away from death?

She wanted to look back at him, to see if his face revealed anything, but she couldn't tear her focus from the arena.

The emperor tossed out a careless hand, as if to sweep away the fighters before him.

Thank the gods. It wasn't the thumb-out gesture that meant death. Velia swallowed hard as relief pulsed through her.

In the arena, the other gladiator helped Achilles to his feet, and they trudged toward opposite exits.

"He survived!" Velia gasped. She finally turned her head to look at Ferox. Her uncle had disappeared at some point; the fight had not been particularly exciting, and he must have had something else to attend to.

"I told you he would," Ferox said, with only a trace of smugness. "He lost, though."

Velia could hardly spare the energy to be displeased at the loss. It wasn't ideal, of course; the more Achilles won, the higher price she could fetch for his appearances. But for his first match, she was happy with survival. And he wasn't even injured, which was another blessing.

As Achilles made it to where they stood, he yanked off his helmet. He, for one, did not look grateful to be alive. Instead, he was scowling, a thunderous expression on his sweaty, red face.

"You did well—" Velia held out a hand to him, but he brushed past her.

Velia took a step to follow him, but Ferox laid a hand on her shoulder.

"Let him go," Ferox said. "He'll want to be alone for a time."

Velia stared after Achilles, now swallowed up by the passage of the arena's back area. "I'm going to arrange another match as soon as possible," she decided aloud. "Within the week, if I can." She'd seen new gladiators defeated in an early match lose all confidence. Sometimes, they never recovered. If she allowed Achilles to wallow for too long, the same could happen to him, and he'd be useless to her.

Ferox nodded. "Good."

His approval pleased her. Now that she no longer had to worry about Achilles—for the moment, at least—a new tendril of unease unfurled within her. "You're up soon, right?"

"After the next two matches."

That could be in as little as half an hour. With an abruptness that surprised even herself, she threw her arms around him, clasping them around his burly middle as tight as she could. "Please don't die," she mumbled.

A chuckle rumbled in his chest next to her ear. His arms came up, hesitant, his fingertips brushing her back before they dropped. "I won't."

She drew back, releasing him. She looked up into his eyes and found his gaze steady. "Is that a promise?"

Velia wasn't sure why she felt so unsettled at the thought of Ferox's imminent appearance in the arena. She'd befriended gladiators before, after all—Jason, Lea, and others. She'd seen them fight, lose, be wounded. Never before had she felt this choking dread, this bone-deep fear they might not come back.

"It's a promise, Velia."

She let out a long sigh, trying to absorb some of his composure. "Good."

12

H ALF AN HOUR LATER, Velia ran her fingers over and over the end of her braid as Ferox stepped into the arena. Lucullus stood next to her. The noise of the crowd rose to a deafening pitch—the loudest today by far, maybe even the loudest Velia had ever heard. The announcer gestured excitedly, but there was no hope of hearing him over the roar of the crowd.

The emperor was on his feet as soon as Ferox appeared. He'd risen a few times before at particularly exciting moments of previous matches, but never had he stood before the fight had even begun. Velia recalled that the emperor had asked for Ferox specifically, having seen him fight in his youth. Ferox truly was the best.

Pride swelled in her chest, warring with the twisting nerves. She was proud of him, and he hadn't even lifted his sword yet.

Ferox's opponent entered the arena to an enthusiastic but less ardent welcome. Velia recognized him from past matches; he was younger than Ferox, closer to Velia's age, but a skilled fighter who'd quickly gained renown in the past year. A worthy opponent for Ferox. Velia bet the younger man would be eager to prove himself against the recently returned legend, to maintain his reputation as one of the top fighters in the city.

The gladiators circled each other for a moment, taking each other's measure. Then, the younger gladiator leaped forward with the first strike. Velia's fingers twisted into the segments of her braid.

Ferox blocked the strike with a powerful shove of his shield that sent his opponent pitching backward before he righted himself. Velia expected Ferox to take advantage of the other man's stumble to strike again, but instead Ferox retreated, resetting his grip on his shield.

They circled each other for another few breaths. Velia dropped her braid, hands clenched into fists. The tie to her braid had fallen, but she couldn't tear her gaze away for long enough to look for it.

She expected Ferox to make the first move this time, but again, he allowed the younger gladiator to strike.

"What's he doing?" Velia hissed as the fight progressed. She kept seeing opportunities for Ferox to overtake the other fighter, moments where the opponent's shield wavered and Ferox could easily have gotten a sword to his throat.

Lucullus slid her a glance with a raised eyebrow. "He's giving the crowd what they want."

Her uncle's words made Velia realize—Ferox wasn't hesitating or missing opportunities. He'd been in control since the beginning. He was carefully crafting a performance that would capture the audience, holding them in an inescapable grasp.

When she first saw him fight at the ludus, she'd thought he didn't have a theatrical bone in his body. Now, she realized she'd been wrong, though Ferox's version of theater was more subtle than the flamboyant moves and showiness some gladiators employed.

In any case, his version was working. Every time the gladiators came together and then separated, the yells and cheers from the audience rose impossibly higher. The emperor himself was shouting, clapping, gesturing as wildly as any other attendee. Velia might have expected him to behave with more dignity, but there was something refreshing in seeing him as wrapped up in the fight as everyone else.

Something in the fight shifted. Ferox's movements lost their circumspect, almost restrained quality. He became vicious, relentless in his attacks, never dropping back, never giving his opponent a moment to catch his breath. Finally, she saw the truth in his name, which meant wild, ferocious, savage. The crowd roared with delight.

Velia blinked, and it was over. The other gladiator had dropped his shield, and Ferox's blade was leveled straight at his throat.

Exhilaration erupted within her. She jumped up and down. "Yes!" she shouted, her voice mingling with the yells of the thousands of spectators.

Her uncle glanced at her, his lips curved in a smile. He was pleased too, even if he was a bit more dignified in showing it.

The crowd chanted Ferox's name. Velia whooped again, unable to hold back her joy. He'd not only survived, but won. Not that she should have expected any different.

Ferox's helmeted head angled up toward the emperor and his retinue. The emperor was still clapping and celebrating along with everyone else, but after a moment, the ruler seemed to remember that he had a job to do. He extended a hand in a closed fist, the gesture for mercy.

Ferox lowered his sword. The other gladiator picked up his shield, and they departed through opposite sides of the arena.

Velia bounced on her toes as Ferox approached. She wanted to leap into his arms, but held back for her uncle's sake.

Lucullus clapped Ferox on the shoulder. "Well done. You pleased the emperor greatly. I could see it even from here."

Ferox nodded respectfully, pulling off his helmet. His skin glistened with sweat, but he was entirely uninjured. "Thank you."

"You did it!" Velia crowed, the elation of his victory still flooding her.

Ferox turned to her. There was reserve in his gaze, which Velia attributed to her uncle's presence. For a moment, she thought he would only nod to her and depart, but then he suddenly bent down, retrieved something on the ground, and stood back up. He reached for her hand and pressed something into it. Warmth flooded her at his touch, dizzying her so she didn't even register what he'd given her.

By the time she recovered herself, he'd already dropped her hand and disappeared, continuing through the passage. Velia looked down at her palm. He'd given her the fallen tie to her braid.

She closed her fingers over the strip of leather. His thoughtfulness bewildered her. He'd just triumphed in his first fight after a long absence, and he'd stopped to pick up her fallen tie, which she herself had hardly noticed.

Her hand tingled where he'd touched her, sparking a wave of heat that settled in her core. Despite her lingering soreness, she wanted him again. Unfortunately, she sensed she'd have to wait a day or two before her body would permit it.

If their coupling was to continue—as she very much hoped it would—they'd have to make some adjustments. She didn't want to spend days after each encounter hobbling around, much less be rendered out of action for further trysts.

Because there definitely would be further trysts, if Velia had anything to say about it.

After the day of games finished, Velia returned to the ludus with her uncle. None of his gladiators had died, all injuries were minor, and many had been victorious. An excellent day overall.

Velia hadn't seen Achilles or Ferox since their matches. She'd leave Achilles alone, as Ferox advised.

But Ferox, she wanted to see.

First, she went to the kitchen to obtain food. In her experience, gladiators often forgot to eat after a match, their appetite sapped by the residual thrill of the fight. She piled a tray high with flatbread, a few hard-boiled eggs, cheese, and figs.

Ferox's door was closed, but light flickered from beneath. She knocked, balancing the tray on one arm. "It's Velia. I brought you some dinner."

Movement sounded within, the hasty rustling of clothing—as if he was dressing. A moment later, the door swung open, revealing Ferox clad in a clean, knee-length tunic.

Velia arched an eyebrow at him as she brought the food in and set it on the tiny table against the wall. "You needn't have dressed. Nothing I haven't seen before," she said playfully.

The light was dim, but not so dark she couldn't see him flush. He must have made it to the baths in the hours since she'd seen him, as his skin appeared scrubbed clean of the sweat and sand that had covered him after his match, and he smelled like herb-fragranced oil.

"You didn't have to bring me food. I could have gotten it myself."

Velia shrugged. "I don't mind." She spoke casually, as if all she'd done was carry out a quick, thoughtless errand. Not as if she'd been thinking about being alone with him all day.

Ferox lifted the tray and brought it over to the bed, balancing it on his knees as he sat. She realized he was making room for her to sit beside him, as he only had one stool at the table.

She sat, crossing one leg beneath her. Her bent knee brushed his thigh, and she felt him stiffen, but he didn't move away.

He began to eat, and the sight of the food made her realize she hadn't eaten all day, too consumed by the anxiety and excitement of the games. She reached out and broke off a piece of bread.

Wordlessly, he separated out half of the food and pushed it toward her.

"The emperor enjoyed watching you fight." Velia peeled a hard-boiled egg, depositing the shell fragments into a corner of the tray. "Did you notice he was on his feet the whole time? He didn't do that for anyone else."

Ferox shrugged. "Lucullus said as much. But I didn't notice."

Velia rolled her eyes. His words had the air of false modesty. "You definitely noticed. At the very least, you saw his reaction at the end. He was cheering loud enough that he's probably gone hoarse."

Ferox reached for a slice of fig. "He did send a generous gift of prize money this afternoon," he admitted.

"How much?"

"Five thousand sestertii."

"Five thousand!" Velia let out a low whistle. "Not bad. I suppose that's what being the emperor's favorite is worth."

"I'm not his favorite," Ferox muttered.

Velia flicked a piece of eggshell at him. "It's a *good* thing, stupid." Being favored by the emperor meant not just fame and money, but also safety. If Ferox were to lose, the emperor would be much less likely to order the death of his favorite. "Anyway, what are you going to spend it on? Maybe some silken tunics? Or a nice golden armband? You could have rubies set into it!" She was only half-joking; he would look very impressive in such finery.

He shook his head, plucking the fragment of shell from his tunic and dropping it back onto the tray. "I'm going to save it. After this is over—after my next two fights—I'm leaving. I only came back because I was barely scraping by after I bought my freedom. But now, with all this money...I could buy a vineyard. Or a farm. Something that will give me a quiet, peaceful life."

Velia's lips tightened at the reminder that Ferox wouldn't be here forever. She didn't like to think of him gone. But that was months away. Maybe this attraction would run its course.

Or maybe he'd change his mind. Maybe she could convince him to stay. They could be an excellent team, after all; if she acquired a few more gladiators, if Ferox lent his experience to train them up, they'd be unstoppable.

That image of the future spread before her, tempting but insubstantial as a reflection on shifting water.

She couldn't dwell on such things. What mattered was the here and now, and Ferox was right here, right now.

He'd finished his half of the food, plus some of her half which she'd left behind. She lifted the empty tray from his lap and set it on the floor, pushing it beneath the bed.

"I can't picture you as a farmer," she murmured. She slid into his lap, looping her arms around his neck. "Or a…whatever they call someone who owns a vineyard."

He tensed for a moment as her weight settled on him, then relaxed, hands finding her waist and pulling her closer. The position stretched her sore hips, reminding her of her body's current unfortunate infirmity.

Luckily, there were things she could do that wouldn't exacerbate her discomfort. She leaned close, allowing her breasts to brush his chest, then captured his mouth in a kiss. He let out a sharp exhale as their lips met. His arms wound tighter around her, pressing her to him. He tasted of the figs he'd ended his meal with, a lingering sweetness on her tongue.

Her hand found his jaw, tilting his face up to hers. Stubble rasped against her fingers. "You didn't find a barbershop after your bath?" she asked. "I bet they would have paid *you* for the privilege of your post-victory shave."

He gave a dismissive grunt. "That's why I didn't go. The bath was a necessity. The shave was not."

She chuckled. He must be the only gladiator she'd ever met who treated fame as if it were a burden.

"If you're determined to be modest, then perhaps you don't want your prize," she said, lips teasing the skin of his throat. Her hand searched downward, seeking the growing thrust of his arousal between them.

"What—prize?" he managed, the words cutting off as her hand closed around his cock through his tunic. "I told you—there was money—"

"Not that." She squeezed gently, relishing the way his eyes fluttered shut. "Something more fun." She slid off his lap, coming to her knees on the floor before him. *He could do with a rug in here*, she reflected as her knees pressed against the hard, cold flagstone floor. She'd have to convince him to use some of his winnings for a few comforts, even if he didn't plan to stay for long.

But she didn't let the prospect of redecorating distract her from her aim. She shifted aside his tunic and wrapped her hand around the hot, hard flesh. He shuddered at her touch. She leaned close, brushing her lips along his length.

"So," she murmured. "Do you want your prize?"

He let out a long, unsteady exhale. "Yes," he hissed.

She took him into her mouth. He groaned as she eased him as deep as she could, stroking him with her tongue. Her forearms braced on his muscled thighs as she withdrew and then sank her mouth down on him once more.

His hand slid into her hair and tightened, pulling to the point of pain. She reached up to tap his rigid fingers. "That hurts," she murmured against him.

He withdrew his hand with a grunt of apology, clenching it into a fist at his side.

She kept going, finding a slow, deliberate rhythm. He was quiet, but she could hear the heightened rasp of his breathing, feel the twitch and shudder when she did something he particularly liked.

"Velia." The word was a taut plea. He was close, she knew, and she didn't stop. A moment later, his hips jerked, and he groaned, the sound as deep as if pulled from the innermost recesses of his chest, as she swallowed him down.

Then he fell back against the bed, breathing hard. He somehow looked more exhausted than he'd appeared after the match earlier, and Velia smiled in satisfaction. She rose to her feet, wincing as her knees stretched, and wiped her mouth.

"You could use a rug in here," she said, not looking for a response in his current state. She took a step toward the door, assuming he wanted to be alone after the events of the day, but he sat up. His hand swept out, lightly clasping hers. "Stay," he murmured.

She blinked at him, momentarily befuddled by the invitation. From what she knew of him, he seemed like the sort of person who relished solitude, and she'd presumed their sleeping together the previous night had been an anomaly.

"If you wish," he added hurriedly, shoulders tensing as if embarrassed.

Her smile returned. "I do wish," she assured him, and slid into the narrow bed next to him. His arms wrapped around her, his shoulder becoming the perfect pillow for her head.

As soon as she was lying down, warm and comfortable in his arms, the stress and excitement of the day turned to exhaustion, and she gratefully abandoned herself to sleep.

13

VELIA WOKE TO A myriad of pleasurable sensations: tingling warmth on her neck, her breast, her waist, with a solid heat behind her. As her awareness slowly returned, the feelings clarified: Ferox's lips nuzzling her neck, his hand skimming up and down her front, his large body tight against her back. Velia stretched and sighed as the last vestiges of sleep dissolved.

She couldn't think of a better way to wake up than with a muscular, aroused gladiator curled around her body.

She stretched again, this time more suggestively, allowing her bottom to make delicious contact with the swell of his arousal. His breath caught. In a swift motion, she found herself flipped onto her back, pinned flat beneath him.

Her surprised giggle was cut short by the hot, hungry press of his mouth on hers. She stretched her arms over his magnificent shoulders. His hand groped downward to find the curve of her breast, and his thumb swept over her nipple, coaxing it to stiffen. The flood of sensation, sharp but exquisite, made her gasp. He growled in her ear. His hand moved lower, finding the crook of her bent knee and pulling it higher, opening her to him.

Her sore hip and thigh stretched—the only thing that could distract her from the pleasure of this awakening. She hesitated, unsure if she wanted to put a stop to this. Ferox was now busily tugging up the folds of her dress. Her inner muscles, though still tender, gave a hopeful twitch.

Her body wanted him, and though she knew their coupling would be highly enjoyable, she didn't fancy repeating yesterday's level of discomfort. Reluctantly, she laid a hand on his chest. "Ferox," she breathed, voice hoarse with her first spoken word of the day.

He paused. "Yes?"

"I don't—I don't want to." The words were difficult to get out, because she *did* want to—just not right now.

"Oh." He rolled off her. "Sorry."

She sat up, combing her fingers through her tangled hair. "I mean, not now. I need another day or so to recover," she confessed.

He propped himself on his elbow. A wrinkle appeared between his brows. "Recover?"

"From...the night before last." Heat rose to her cheeks.

He blinked at her, uncomprehending.

"Our coupling," she clarified. "I was a little sore after."

She could tell when understanding set in, because it dropped a dark cloud over his expression. A moment later, he was out of the bed, pacing to the other side of the small room. "You mean to say..." His hand clenched into a fist, bracing against the wall. "I hurt you?"

Velia swung her legs out of the bed. "That's not what I said."

He half-turned, his eyes dark and heated. "I knew this was a mistake. From the first moment I wanted you, I knew I should keep my distance. I knew I would hurt you."

The revelation that he'd desired her for longer than she'd realized was interesting, but Velia set it aside for the moment. She rose to her feet and crossed her arms over her chest. She wasn't about to indulge this fit of self-reproach, but she understood where his guilt was coming from. "It was nothing, Ferox. I didn't even notice it then. It was only when I woke up the next morning."

"Tell me how," he demanded, his voice rough. "Tell me how I hurt you. Did I…did I make you bleed?"

"No!" she exclaimed. "It was just a little soreness in my, well, you know. And my legs were a bit stretched from that position we tried. And…" She debated withholding this next piece of information, but he'd asked. "There were some bruises on my hips."

He made a pained noise low in his throat. "I *bruised* you?"

"It's nothing," she insisted. "Look." She gathered up her dress, raising it to waist level.

He turned hesitantly, as if about to face some horrifying carnage. His eyes locked onto the thin marks, now faded to yellow shadows.

She brushed her hand over them. "Nothing," she repeated. She dropped her dress, covering herself to the ankle. "I've gotten worse from bumping my elbow on a doorframe."

Even though she'd covered herself, he was still frozen, disgust and self-loathing written plain on his face. "I'm—sorry," he finally bit out.

She sighed. For a moment, she regretted bringing this up, but she'd planned on raising it with him anyway. "There's nothing to apologize for."

"I've lain with other women," he said, his voice low. "Do you think…did I hurt them too?"

His concern for the women of his past was endearing. "Were they prostitutes?"

He gave a swift nod, his gaze on the floor.

"Then I'd wager all the emperor's money that you were probably one of their best." She approached him, laying a hand on his arm. "Come here." She drew him over to the bed, sat him down, and slid into his lap, sitting sideways across him. His arm curled around her waist to steady her. She kissed his forehead, lips brushing a faded scar. "Do you think I would have brought you dinner if I was displeased with you? Much less spent the night?"

He leaned his head against her shoulder. "No," he grunted, a reluctant admission.

"And do you remember last night, when I told you that you were pulling my hair, and you stopped?" She drew back to meet his gaze. "That's what I would have done, had I noticed any discomfort when we were together. And you would have stopped." She raked a gentle hand through his short hair. "You must trust me in this, as I trust you."

At her words, some of the tension finally eased from his gaze. "I do trust you."

Her stomach gave a strange leap. No one had ever told her that before, and she realized what a great, precious gift it was. She dropped a quick, sweet kiss on his lips, then pulled back, smiling. "It was partly my fault, anyway. I fear that position we tried was a little too ambitious."

"I could teach you some stretches. If you wish to attempt it again."

Velia giggled. "Next you'll have me running laps with Achilles."

He snorted.

"I was probably just out of practice," she said. "It had been a while since I'd…" She gave an expressive shrug.

"Well," he replied, sliding his hands up her back, "that's an easy fix." His lips found a spot on her neck that made her gasp and clutch at him.

"Mm," she breathed. "It may take a great deal of experimentation to find the perfect way to lie together."

"Once you're feeling better, I'm at your disposal for as long as it takes," he murmured, then captured her mouth with his.

Later that day, Velia returned to the ludus after paying another visit to Oppius. The official had once again extolled the virtues of his bachelor nephew, but eventually Velia succeeded in booking Achilles for his next fight at the end of the week. She'd also received the remaining money due for his first appearance. She wished she could have negotiated his fee higher, but that wouldn't happen until he'd logged a few wins and built some popularity.

Still, her half of the fee was more money than she made in a week from her uncle, though she still had to pay him back for Achilles's room and feeding.

She would do that first. After passing through the gate, Velia headed toward the building that housed her uncle's office.

A voice from behind caught her attention. "Velia?"

She turned to see Jason. He appeared to have just come from a training session, bare-chested and sweaty, with a damp rag laid over his shoulder.

"Can I have a word?" he asked.

"Of course." She had always liked Jason; he had a mild, reasonable personality, and he wasn't bad to look at either. His features were refined, but a previously broken nose lent his face a rugged edge. His body was lithe and well-proportioned, skin tanned to a golden hue by hours spent training in the sun. Before Ferox arrived, Jason had often been the target of her ogling, though she'd never felt anything close to the pull toward him that she felt with Ferox.

Jason scrubbed the rag over his face, mopping up some lingering sweat. "You've been spending time with Ferox."

"Has he told you?" Though Ferox seemed like a private person, she might have expected he'd speak of their encounters to his closest friend.

Jason shook his head swiftly. "Of course not. But I have eyes. As does Lea."

Ah, that was it—Lea had seen her yesterday morning.

She dipped her head to concede the point. "What of it?"

He took a step closer, lowering his voice though there was no one nearby. "I hope this doesn't offend you, Velia, but...I know in the past, you've seen fit to be rather, well, *free* with your...favors."

Velia's eyebrows shot up. "Where exactly is this conversation going?"

Jason raised his hands in a conciliatory gesture. "I mean no offense. I only wanted to say…Ferox isn't like that. He doesn't, well, he doesn't share that part of himself lightly."

Velia had sensed that, but still she frowned. "He's been with others."

"Yes, but as far as I know, always courtesans. Those encounters are like buying lunch from a food stall. And they were infrequent at best. Only the night before matches."

Velia tried to understand what Jason was getting at. "So you think your friend is too good for me, is that it? Because I'm just some…some *slut* who's leading him astray—"

"No!" Jason's exclamation cut her off. "That's not at all what I meant."

He seemed genuine, his expression radiating sincerity and dismay at her interpretation of his words, but her lips pressed together. A familiar insult echoed in her mind: *stupid whore.*

"I just wanted you to understand that if he's…spending time with you in that way…he doesn't do it lightly." Jason's gaze, serious and dark, held hers.

The earnest tenor of his voice assuaged some of the tightness in her chest. "I see," she murmured.

"I only ask that you take care," Jason continued. "You must know he doesn't intend to stay here past the end of the games. I won't have him leaving broken-hearted again."

Velia cocked her head. "What do you mean, again? Was there someone else?" It seemed to contradict what Jason had said earlier about Ferox's lack of previous entanglements.

"No. Not like that." He hesitated, eyes sweeping up to the sky and back down to her face. "We had a friend. He died in the arena. Ferox took it very hard because—" He stopped himself. "Forgive me. It's not my story to tell. Anyway, that's why he left."

Velia made a murmur of acknowledgment, turning this new information over in her mind. She had wondered why Ferox left and why he'd been so reluctant to return.

"I have no wish to hurt him," she said after a moment. "We both know this won't last forever. But if you're asking me to stay away from him…I can't promise that."

Jason shook his head. "No. I only wanted you to understand. To be careful. And"—a crooked grin lit his face—"if you have any mercy on me, *please* don't tell him I spoke of this to you. He'll smother me in my sleep."

Velia chuckled. "I won't."

"Thank you." Jason nodded to her and stepped aside.

Velia continued on her way, mulling over Jason's words. If Jason was correct that Ferox had only lain with women the night before his fights, that meant him asking her to stay last night truly was unusual. Not to mention their abbreviated tryst this morning.

For there was no match today he needed distraction from. That seemed to mean he desired her in a different way than he'd ever wanted a woman before.

Velia had to admit the same might be true for herself. She hadn't been truly tempted by anyone since coming to the ludus, her previous urges toward recklessness tempered by the new and fulfilling life she found here.

Maybe this was uncharted territory for them both. After all, she knew what it was like to have transitory encounters—one boy here, another there. But this feeling of wanting the same man over and over again…this was entirely new.

Velia reached her uncle's office, paid him what he was due, then spent the rest of the afternoon busy with other errands. Messages needed to be taken, there was a supply delivery to oversee, and the physician had to be summoned to check on one of the men who'd sustained a mild injury in yesterday's games.

As the day came to an end, Velia stole a moment to herself in her room, sitting on her bed with a grateful sigh as she rested her tired feet.

A knock sounded at her door. She grimaced, but heaved herself to her feet and opened the door.

Her exhaustion was quickly forgotten as she beheld Ferox standing in the hallway outside her room. She smiled, opening the door wider. "Hello."

He murmured a greeting, then thrust something at her. "For you."

Velia took the object, a palm-sized clay container. "What's this?" She removed the cover, finding a thick ointment within. A minty fragrance mixed with something herbal spiraled to her nose.

"Henbane seeds and peppermint," he explained. "It helps with sore muscles. I thought…it would make you feel better."

"Oh!" Befuddlement made her stammer. "You—you didn't have to do that."

"I know."

"I mean, thank you," she managed, flushing. She was woefully unpracticed at the niceties of accepting gifts.

He ducked his head in a nod of acknowledgment and turned to leave.

Velia held up a hand, fighting through the mental disarray his kind gesture had produced. "Wait—I have something for you too." She slipped into her room, set the ointment container on a shelf, and retrieved Ferox's half of the money from Oppius. "I booked another fight on Friday," she informed him as she dropped the silver coins into his hand. "How was Achilles today?"

Ferox shrugged. "Irritating, but that's nothing new. It's good for a novice to lose early. Stops them from thinking they're invincible."

"Did you lose your first fight?"

He shook his head. "But I lost the second and drew the third. After that, I understood how hard I'd have to work."

It was difficult to imagine Ferox losing. Maybe one day, someone would think of Achilles the same way. She could only hope.

"I'll leave you to rest," Ferox said, then turned toward his own room.

For a moment, she debated calling him back, inviting him to stay, but after Jason's warning earlier, she wondered if a bit of distance might benefit them. She'd never had someone show so much care toward her. Her gaze lingered on the little container of ointment he'd brought. *How sweet.*

Jason's warning had been delivered with Ferox in mind, but Velia now realized she might need to look out for herself as well. There was no future in this, after all. This dalliance could be a pleasant diversion for the next two months, but that was it. Ferox would leave, and she had to prepare herself to let him go.

14

FEROX STOOD BESIDE VELIA as they watched Achilles's second fight. Achilles was holding his own against his new opponent, and this fight had already lasted longer than the first one.

Ferox kept one eye on Achilles and the other on Velia. She anxiously ran her hands over and over the length of her braid, draped over her shoulder. With each pass, the leather tie at the bottom loosened.

When it finally fell, tumbling down her chest, Ferox's hand snapped out to catch it. He held it out to her, but she paid him no attention, eyes locked on the fight. Ferox closed his fingers around the strip of leather. She'd eventually notice it was missing, and he could give it back to her then.

He had seen relatively little of her in the past few days. Both of them had been kept busy, Velia with her uncle's business and Ferox with preparing Achilles for his next fight. In her free time, Velia supervised Achilles's training sessions, but there was something hesitant in her manner toward him. It was strange, after how forward she'd been previously. In Velia, hesitation apparently looked like *not* propositioning him in the middle of a banquet or inviting herself into his room and doing wicked things to him with her mouth.

On Ferox's part, his longing had only increased. The two nights he'd spent with her seemed to have altered something within him, knocking loose whatever had stoppered this deep well of craving. It was unaccountable, the way he wanted her. He'd never slept beside someone before, let alone two nights in a row. He *liked* her—but it had to be more than that. After all, he liked Lea and Jason, but he'd never been driven to sleep with his body curled around either of them, had he?

There was also the fact that those two nights had been the best sleep he'd gotten since returning to the ludus, and perhaps even before. Velia must be some sort of talisman, keeping Hector's shade at bay. Each of the nights since, by contrast, he'd woken with a pounding heart, visions of Hector's death spiraling behind his eyelids.

But even if Velia didn't protect him from the dreams, he'd still want her so badly it hurt.

She'd been so diffident lately, though, and he had no idea how to raise the matter. How did one go about asking a woman to lie with him?

Velia let out a shocked yelp, and Ferox hastily returned his attention to the fight.

"Yes!" Velia crowed. Achilles, taking advantage of his left-handedness, had managed to get his sword behind the other man's shield and deal a deep cut to his upper chest. It was exactly the maneuver Ferox had taught him, and pride filled him.

The man stumbled back, a gleam of blood catching the sunlight. The crowd whooped and hooted at the successful strike.

Achilles paused for a moment, as if surprised he'd actually done it.

The other fighter glanced down at his chest, likely assessing whether it was worth surrendering or if he could fight on.

"Come on, give up," Velia hissed.

But the opponent renewed his grip on his sword and launched himself forward with another attack, this time adjusting the position of his shield to block further incursions from the same angle.

They fought on. Achilles managed to keep himself in one piece, but couldn't land another strike on the man's body. Ferox could see both fighters tiring. Their movements slowed, their feet dragging through the sand. Sweat shone on their shoulders and backs.

The crowd, too, was losing energy. The cheers at each attack grew fainter. Ferox glanced at where the emperor sat and found the ruler turned away from the fight, in conversation with one of his entourage.

"Do something!" Velia shouted, though there was no way Achilles could hear her. She hopped up and down in frustration.

Ferox already sensed how this was going to end. The official stepped forward, gesturing with his hands and saying something that caused the fighters to halt. The opponent bent over, bracing his hands on his knees as he drew in gulping breaths. Achilles scrubbed a hand over his face, shoulders slumping in exhaustion.

"A draw?" Velia demanded in outrage.

Ferox slid her a glance. "Better than a loss, no?"

A muscle in her jaw pulsed. "He was supposed to win."

"He did well. He lasted a while and didn't get himself injured."

As the fighters trudged toward opposite exits, Velia tore her gaze from the arena and whirled toward him. "He wasn't aggressive enough. He missed too many opportunities. I've seen the way you're training him. You spend too much time having him run and lift weights. He needs more practice sparring."

Ferox raised his eyebrows, taking a step toward her. "Are you criticizing my training methods?"

She met his gaze, her blue-gray eyes hot with frustration. "Maybe I am."

He folded his arms over his chest. "You know many things, Velia, but not what it's like to be out there." He jerked his head toward the arena. "At this stage, stamina and strength are what will keep him alive. And no matter how much I teach him, nothing we do in the training yard can replicate what it's like with thousands of people watching you, cheering for you to win or lose. Maybe even calling for your death. We can practice from dawn till dusk, but part of his training will only come from experience."

Velia opened her mouth, and he sensed a sharp retort coming, but she fell silent as the subject of their discussion reached them. Achilles was sandy and red-faced, walking with heavy steps, helmet tucked under one arm. He shouldered his way between them without a word.

"You did well!" Velia called after him. "Next time you'll surely win!"

Ferox was impressed by how much enthusiasm she imbued her voice with, and glad of it, as Achilles deserved the encouragement.

Achilles turned briefly, acknowledged her words with a jerk of his head, then continued on his way.

Velia let out a sigh and leaned against the wall behind her. Her hand went back to her braid, but as her fingers smoothed over it, she paused and glanced down.

Ferox knew what she'd noticed and held out the fallen tie.

She chuckled and took it from him. "Thank you." She began to braid the locks that had loosened. "I'm sorry. I didn't mean to question you. If anyone knows what they're doing, it's you."

The brief tension of their argument evaporated like a drop of water on a hot stove. He liked that she didn't cling to disagreements.

Ferox accepted her apology with a nod, his gaze drawn to the way her deft fingers wove through her hair. The practiced motions rekindled the desire that Achilles's fight had momentarily distracted him from. He remembered what those slender, skilled hands felt like on him—grasping his shoulders, tangled in his hair, stroking his cock.

A shiver of need passed over him. He couldn't go another night without her. He had to have her in his bed, beneath him, atop him, however she'd have him.

She took a step in the direction Achilles had gone. Instinctively, his body moved to block her, as if thwarting an opponent's advance in the arena.

She halted and glanced up at him with a raised eyebrow. "Was there something else?"

He backed up a step, regretting the brutish maneuver. He knew little about courting women, but he was fairly certain one wasn't supposed to obstruct their path as if defending against another gladiator.

"Yes," he admitted. His jaw worked, struggling to summon the right thing to say. She deserved poetry, elegant words strung together like pearls, but he had none. He had only the simple truth of his need for her. "Velia, I wondered if…That is, I wanted to—I thought you might—"

She cocked her head, a cool, expectant smile on her lips. "Yes?" The knowing look in her eyes scrambled the few words he'd managed to call forth.

"I need you," he finally ground out. "Tonight." The words sounded much harsher than he wished. Dis, what was he thinking, to demand this of her like some sort of beast? But to him, it wasn't a demand, but a confession. A plea.

"If you'll have me," he added hastily, hoping to temper the bluntness of his words.

The coolness left her expression, replaced by an eager heat that sparked in her gaze. For some inconceivable reason, she looked pleased at his words. As if it gratified her that his longing rendered him incapable of basic civility.

"I will have you," she murmured. The dark promise in her words sent a quiver of anticipation through him. He couldn't help glancing at the sky, estimating how many hours remained until dark. Until she would be in his bed once more. Nightfall couldn't come soon enough.

15

VELIA'S KNUCKLES RAPPED AGAINST Ferox's door in a quick, eager pattern. She'd been looking forward to this all day. Jason's warning earlier that week had made her hesitate, and she'd decided not to make another advance until Ferox did. Or until she couldn't stand it anymore.

Luckily, Ferox had succumbed first, and how could she refuse when he said "I need you" in that wicked growl?

Barely a moment after she knocked, the door swung open. She smiled at him and took a step into the room—but stopped short.

The floor looked different. Darker, lumpier, indistinct in the flickering light of the single lamp. "What's this?"

She took a tentative step forward. Her feet sank into something soft.

"You said I needed a rug," he replied. "I bought three."

A shocked laugh bubbled up. "You did?" He'd been undone, shattered in the aftermath of their last encounter. She hadn't even realized he'd heard her offhand comment about the rug, much less expected him to go out and purchase not one, but *three*. The rugs were clumsily layered over each other, covering as much of the floor as possible.

"They don't match," he warned her. "They look hideous in daylight."

She snorted. In the low light, she could only make out hints of color and pattern. "What possessed you to get three of them?"

"I realized why you said that. I wasn't sure one would be soft enough."

How was she supposed to withstand this? In the last week alone, he'd brought her ointment to soothe sore muscles, safeguarded the tie to her hair when it fell, and now he'd bought *three* rugs simply because she'd mentioned it. Jason had warned her about playing with Ferox's heart, but if this kept up, her own would be lost to him all too soon.

If it's not already.

"Well," Velia said. "I suppose we'd better test them out." She reached for him, pulling his tunic over his head. His body was bare beneath, his cock already thickening.

She dropped to her knees. "Very nice," she murmured approvingly as her knees sank into the three layers of padding.

Velia took hold of his cock, giving it one stroke to bring him to full attention. He drew in a sharp breath at the touch of her hand, which turned into a groan as she closed her lips around him. His hand went to her head, but this time he didn't tangle his fingers in her hair, only allowed his fingertips to graze the back of her head.

She released him from her mouth. "I could do this all day." Her lips brushed him as she spoke, and his hand twitched where it laid on her head.

He made a strained noise. "I fear I'm going to disappoint you."

She chuckled, then slid her mouth down his length once more. It really was more comfortable this way—but he didn't give her long to enjoy it.

"Velia," he hissed after the next stroke. He took a step back, pulling away, and then he tugged her to her feet, stripped off her dress, and turned her toward the bed.

He grabbed the pillow resting at the head of the bed and tossed it aside, pointing to the spot it had occupied. "There," he said. "Kneel. Put your hands on the wall."

She raised her eyebrows, intrigued, and did as he asked. What did he have in mind? She was facing away from him. Did he mean to take her from behind?

She quickly figured it out as he lay flat on the bed and slid his face beneath her spread thighs. "Oh!"

His tongue opened her, his lips latching onto that sweet place at the apex of her quim.

The onslaught of sensation made her shudder. His hands wrapped around her thighs, anchoring her to him.

"Can you breathe?" she gasped.

"Don't. Care," came the muffled response.

His tongue was doing something to her that made her hips rock, seeking more. In this position, she had more control over the angle of connection. She braced her hands against the wall, arching her back to find the perfect position. A moan tore from her lips. He growled in response, the sound vibrating through her.

His lips pulled and teased at her. She matched his rhythm with the roll of her hips, each breathless movement driving her pleasure higher.

A quiver rippled over her, and her internal muscles clenched. She raised herself off him, just enough to enjoy the suspended pleasure, dark and bittersweet. Her hands trembled where they pressed against the wall, her body urging her to relax back down onto him, to let him finish what he'd started.

He lifted his head, seeking her with his mouth, but she moved herself higher. "No," she sighed. "Not yet." She wanted to feel what it was like to climax with him inside her, his cock stretching and filling her.

She maneuvered down his body until her thighs clasped his hips, his arousal swelling in front of her.

His hands settled on her waist. "Gods, Velia, I've been imagining this ever since you told me that story about—about how you ended up here."

She giggled when she realized what he was referring to: the tale of how her parents had caught her tumbling a man. "Really? Me getting caught with another man is what you fantasize about?"

"Not the getting caught," he clarified. "And certainly not the other man. But you atop me like this…" His hands slid lower, taking hold of her hips. "Riding me…"

Her breath hitched at the naked lust in his voice. She liked the thought of him imagining her, being the object of his fantasies. "I told you that in one of our first conversations. Have you been thinking of me all this time? Before we even kissed?" She wrapped a hand around his cock and gave him a languid stroke.

"Yes," he hissed.

"And do you do this while you think of me?" She passed her hand over him once more, fingers playing along his length.

"Velia, please," he groaned. "Don't make me admit that."

She arched an eyebrow. "It's nothing to be ashamed of. I've done the same. After our first kiss, for example."

He made another noise of desperation. "You can't—can't tell me those things while you have your hand wrapped around my cock."

She decided to have pity on him—besides, her own body was still quivering with lust—and raised herself over him, notching him at her entrance. Slowly, she slid down, taking him inch by inch. "Oh, that's good," she moaned as she settled onto him.

His fingers clenched on her hips, digging into her flesh. His eyes were squeezed shut tight, face frozen in an expression of utter torment. She braced her hands on his chest and arched her back, taking him deeper. Primed as she was, every movement sent licks of heat through her. She had a feeling this would not last long for either of them.

His hands were gripping her so tightly she winced. She didn't mind his greedy, possessive clasp, but after their first encounter, she knew he wouldn't like it if he ended up bruising her again. "Ferox," she murmured. "Your hands."

He released her with a grunt. "Sorry. I shouldn't be allowed to touch you at all."

His words sparked an idea, devious and tempting. She glanced around, noting her dress on the floor within reach of the bed. Then, her eyes lit on a small metal hook driven into the wall above the bed, perhaps once used to hang a lamp. "Perhaps you shouldn't."

She anchored one hand on the bed and stretched her other arm down, until her fingertips brushed the fabric of her dress, just able to catch it without leaving him. She untangled the fabric sash from the folds of the dress. "Give me your hands."

He looked at her with a suspicious gleam in his eyes, but complied. She wound the length of fabric around his wrists, securing it with a knot. Then, she leaned forward and drew his arms up, until the fabric caught on the hook over his head. The position left him sitting against the wall, arms stretched above. It presented an extremely appealing sight, with the powerful muscles of his arms taut and bunched, yet helpless.

He craned his head to stare at the hook dubiously. "You know that won't hold me."

She rolled her eyes. "Stop bragging. I know." She had no doubt he was strong enough to rip the hook from the plaster wall if he chose, and even without brute force, only a little dexterity would be required to slip the fabric free of it. "But you're going to let it hold you, because I want you to."

She gripped his shoulders and sank back down onto him. He let out a hiss. His arms tensed, and she feared her little scheme was over already; she could envision the hook being pulled out of the wall as easily as one might pluck a flower from the ground.

But either it held, or Ferox mastered himself. The thought that he was allowing her to toy with him like this, that he'd accept restraint even when he was more than capable of freeing himself simply because she wanted it this way—it sent a fresh cascade of desire through her.

She moved atop him, rocking her hips back and forth in the way that brought her the greatest pleasure. "See how gentle this can be?" she whispered breathlessly.

The muscles of his stomach tensed, rippling. "It doesn't feel gentle to me," he ground out. "It feels like agony."

"But you're happy to suffer for me, aren't you?"

He let out a defeated groan. The pleasure was mounting, and Velia needed more. Her hand slipped from his shoulder and slid between her legs.

His dark, hungry gaze tracked her movements. "I could help you with that if I had my hands free."

She managed a chuckle despite the lust threatening to overwhelm her. "The way you look right now is helping me plenty." She stroked herself in tight, firm circles, feeling her inner muscles twitch.

He growled as she clenched around him. "Velia, this is going to kill me."

Her eyes fell shut, brow furrowing in concentration as she chased the pleasure hovering just out of reach. He shuddered beneath her. His breath grated through his teeth. The evidence of his barely controlled desire finally undid her. The climax burst upon her, and her body bowed and arched atop him as she wrested every bit of pleasure she could from it.

When it released its grip on her, she collapsed forward, catching herself against his upright torso, his chest warm and unyielding. He bent his head to kiss the top of hers, lips brushing her hair.

Once some control of her muscles returned, she eased herself off of him, replacing the clasp of her body with her hand. A tremor rippled through him, bound hands yanking at the restraints. The hook creaked and wiggled, but didn't give way.

She slid her hand up and down his length. She might have taken him in her mouth, but that would have deprived her of the sight of him gasping and quivering, an alluring combination of raw masculine power and helplessness.

His breathing grew harsh and ragged as she stroked him. A moan tore from his lips, taking the vague shape of her name. The sound sent a dark shock of residual pleasure through her. She knew he must be painfully close, so it didn't surprise her when after only a few passes of her hand, his hips bucked. His seed jetted over her fingers as his body went rigid.

A cracking noise sounded, and Velia glanced up to see that the hook had partially yielded. The surrounding plaster splintered, dust and fragments tumbling down the wall. The hook remained in the wall, but canted downward at an angle.

"Oops," Velia said with a satisfied grin. "We'll have to fix that."

Ferox didn't seem capable of speech, but Velia took pity on him and reached up to unhook his bound wrists, then untied them. She fetched a rag, wiped her hands, then cleaned the remains of his seed from him as well. Once those practicalities were accomplished, she slid back into bed with him.

His arms closed around her. "I didn't mind that, but I missed touching you." His voice was low and tender.

She snuggled into his chest with a pleased sigh. She felt similarly; though there had been an undeniable thrill in toying with him like that, the pleasure of being held in his arms was like no other.

Beneath her ear, his heart still pounded, but gradually, as the quiet moments stretched, it slowed. Her breathing matched his, and she allowed it to lull her to sleep.

16

VELIA WOKE BEFORE FEROX in the morning. The blanket had fallen off them in the night, but the heat of Ferox's body rendered it entirely superfluous. She'd spent the night enveloped in his arms, her head pillowed on his chest.

Her eyes caught the riot of color spread over the floor. She smiled. He was right about the rugs; they were hideous in daylight, all clashing patterns and incongruous colors. But she loved the chaotic disorder for what it represented.

She squinted up at the small window high in the wall. The sky was still gray, as if just past dawn. That meant if Ferox roused himself in good time, they could squeeze in another coupling before having to rise.

She gave a luxurious stretch, allowing her bottom to make contact with his hips. He stirred, and the arm that lay over her waist tightened. She loved the way he held her, as if she was so precious that he needed to keep her with him even in sleep.

Behind her, she felt his cock beginning to thicken. She slid a hand back to help it along. A sleepy shudder ran through him as she took hold of it, and his hips pressed forward, giving even more of him to her touch.

The rhythm of his breathing changed, and his hand skimmed from her waist to find her bare breasts, fingertips grazing her nipples.

"Did I wake you?" she asked innocently.

He let out a rumbly groan. His breath caught as he reached full arousal, filling her hand with warm stiffness. The place between her legs throbbed, not satisfied for long even after last night's intense climax.

"You want me again?" he murmured in her ear.

She nodded eagerly. "Quickly, though," she said, eyeing the increasing lightness of the sky.

"That won't be a problem." From behind, his hand palmed between her thighs. He made a low, hungry noise when his fingers slipped in the wetness that had already gathered. He stroked her gently, fingers testing and exploring. "Is there pain?"

"No." She grinned, though he couldn't see her face. "You were very gentle last night."

"Not like I had a choice," he growled. His thumb found the spot that made her shudder, and he circled it slowly. Pleasure flared at his touch, and she bent her knee forward, opening herself to him.

"Take me like this," she said breathlessly.

He considered for a moment as he stroked her with the flat of his broad thumb. "Like this?" He moved his hand to her hip, holding her in place. His cock slid between her thighs and nudged against her sex.

"Yes," she breathed.

He moved against her again. Though he wasn't penetrating her, heat still kindled at the blunt, warm press of him. His bottom arm slid beneath her torso, elbow bent to splay his hand over her chest in a possessive grasp.

She waited expectantly for him to enter her, but he only kept up that maddening slide against her. She arched her back, hoping to guide him where she wanted, but he evaded her movements. That was when she realized he was doing this on purpose—retaliation for how she'd toyed with him last night.

"I want you inside me," she purred, trying to make the words sound as seductive as possible. Surely, few men could resist hearing something like that.

He chuckled in her ear. "That wouldn't be very gentle, would it?"

Apparently, Ferox was one of the few. "I don't care about gentle!" she protested.

"I do." His hips rocked against her bottom, the friction of his cock slick and delicious. "You were adamant that you needed to be treated more delicately."

"I never said that." She arched against him once more, to no avail.

"In any case…" His hand slid between her legs, pinning his cock even tighter against her. The increased pressure made her squirm, and he let out a groan. "This is"—his breath hitched—"enough."

"Not for me," she complained, though she loved that her body could bring him pleasure without him even being inside her.

"Velia, if I go inside you, I'm going to spill immediately," he warned. "And I don't think you want that."

She huffed. He was right; the risk of pregnancy was too great, despite her stockpile of helpful herbs. She realized there might be more to his devious teasing than the desire to torment her. He was trying to be as prudent as possible in their encounters.

"Fine," she conceded.

"Good girl," he murmured. The words sent a dark spiral of pleasure through her, only heightening her need. "Why don't you touch yourself for me?"

She stretched a hand down, her fingers quickly finding her most sensitive spot. Desire mounted as she stroked, and her muscles tensed. He kept up his rhythmic movements against her, and each thrust wound her tighter, drove her higher.

"Is this what you do when you think of me?" His voice was unsteady, hoarse. "Is this how you touch yourself?"

"Well, there's not usually a man behind me, sliding his cock between my legs," she answered with as much wryness as she could muster.

He let out a short laugh, a burst of heat on her neck. "I should hope not."

"This is better," she clarified, in case there was any doubt. "*Much* better." She rocked with him, the feeling different from when he was inside her. It was gentler, softer, but the sensation had a pull to it, a keenness that tugged her inexorably toward climax.

A tremor rippled through her. The tight ball of need contracted. She moaned, the sound high and desperate.

"Come for me, Velia," he growled, and she shattered. His arm tightened around her chest, holding her in place as she quaked and writhed. Her head flung back, making contact with his shoulder, and incoherent noises burst from her mouth.

Behind her, he shuddered, breath hissing through his teeth. His hips bucked against her, rough and wild, and then he groaned.

He fell back a moment later, finally releasing his hold on her. She allowed herself to collapse backward as well, sprawling over his body. They were both breathing hard, and Velia felt sweat on her forehead despite the coolness of the morning. She stared up at the blank white ceiling as Ferox lazily stroked her hair. Soon, his movements became more purposeful, and she realized he wasn't stroking her hair, but braiding it to prepare for the day.

She sighed, half in pleasure at his touch and half in resignation at the thought of removing herself from his bed. With him, she felt spoiled, cared for, cherished in a way she never had, and that blissful sensation would evaporate as soon as she got up. But noises—footsteps, the clatter of doors opening and closing—already sounded from outside, so the day would have to begin.

Ferox eyed Velia as they watched Achilles's third fight. Watching her was almost more exciting than the match itself. She alternately jumped up and down, clenched her fists, chewed her nails, and shouted unintelligibly at the combatants. Her antics were quite entertaining, but Ferox dragged his focus back to the fight.

At some point in this match, Achilles would attempt a maneuver they'd been practicing for the past week, and Ferox was eager to see if it would pay off in a win. He wanted to give Velia the victory she craved. Achilles's greatest strength, for now, was his left-handedness, but they hadn't been exploiting it to maximum effect.

Achilles wasn't yet well-known among the other combatants, so Ferox had decided to employ the element of surprise. He'd taught Achilles to begin the match with his sword in his right hand, and lull his opponent into a false sense of security with a clumsy start. Then, at the proper moment, he'd swap sword and shield, putting the sword in his left hand, and take the offensive.

It was risky; if Achilles fumbled the switch, he could find himself disarmed and unprotected. In some similar instances, the official would pause the match and allow a fighter to reset his equipment, but it could just as easily lead to a loss, possibly with a serious injury.

So Ferox had drilled Achilles over and over again on the swap until he was fairly sure the novice could execute it in his sleep.

Ferox kept his gaze on Achilles, sensing it would happen soon. He prayed the novice wouldn't lose his nerve and try to conduct the whole fight with his right hand. That would surely herald a disastrous loss.

When his opponent stumbled, Achilles darted backward a step instead of pressing forward. Ferox held his breath. Sunlight flashed on the blade of Achilles's sword, and when Ferox blinked, the weapon was in the novice's left hand, the shield in his right.

Ferox let out his breath. Achilles had done it as perfectly as he'd ever done it in practice. The crowd roared at the daring maneuver. Even the emperor was paying attention, leaning forward against the balustrade in his section.

This trick would only work once, but if it secured Achilles's first victory, it would be worth it.

Achilles's opponent was flustered by the switch, and struggled to defend against the unexpected angle of attack. Achilles drove the man backward, shoving him off balance with a sideways thrust of his shield.

Velia shrieked. "Come on! This is it!"

The opponent staggered. In trying to catch himself, he lost his grip on his shield, which thumped to the sand. Achilles's sword flashed out, its tip at the opponent's throat.

The other fighter dropped his sword and raised his hands in surrender. The crowd thundered with cheers and applause.

"Yes!" Velia screeched, jumping up and down. She threw herself into Ferox's arms, hugging him with rib-crushing force. "You did it!"

He allowed himself to return the embrace, lifting her off her feet. Her joy seemed to diffuse into him, and for a moment he wanted nothing more than to give her a thousand victories.

But their time was limited, he reminded himself as he set her back down. The games were nearly half over. Ferox would fight his second match the week after next, and then there would only be a month remaining.

One more month with Velia. Far too little.

He wondered if Hector's ghost was getting irritated at being unable to haunt him when he spent each night with Velia. Ferox still wasn't sure what sort of power she had, but it hadn't waned. Maybe the ghost would lose interest and move on. Or maybe Hector was getting angrier and angrier at being deprived of a mind to torment. Maybe he'd be so angry he'd follow Ferox wherever he went after this.

The thought made dread creep down his spine, but Ferox forced himself to return his attention to the arena. Achilles was now strutting around the sand, sword raised, as he soaked up the cheers of the spectators. He pulled off his helmet, exposing his flame-red hair, which somehow drove the cheers even higher.

Ferox rolled his eyes. "He wins one match and thinks he's Mars himself. He's going to be insufferable after this."

"Oh, let him enjoy it," Velia said. "He deserves it. Some gladiators actually enjoy their fame, you know."

Ferox grunted. He didn't want to admit it, but witnessing Achilles's first victory gave him a strange gratification. The emperor was entertained, the crowd was cheering, Velia was thrilled—all because of the days and weeks Ferox had devoted to training the novice.

His mind turned again to what would happen after the games were over, the quiet life he'd seek in Hispania, far from the ghosts of the ludus.

Would anything in that life give him this feeling of proud satisfaction?

And what about Velia? Would he spend the rest of his days missing her touch, her laugh, even her constantly disintegrating braid?

It doesn't matter. Velia might make his present circumstances bearable, enjoyable even, but that was as far as it went. When the time came, he would leave her behind.

No matter how much it hurt.

17

THE NEXT DAY, VELIA carried two pouches of coin over to where Ferox and Achilles were taking a break in the shade of the colonnaded portico. She tossed one to each of them. "Your winnings," she said to Achilles. "And your share of the fee," she said to Ferox.

Achilles eagerly dumped a handful of the shining silver coins into his palm. "How much?"

"Five hundred."

He made a noise of appreciation. "Not bad."

Velia glanced at Ferox. "Better not tell him how much you got after your win."

Achilles slid the coins back into the pouch. "How much?"

"Five thousand," Ferox said.

Achilles swore.

"That's what you have to look forward to," Velia informed him. "Keep winning."

He cast Ferox a dark, jealous look, then tightened the tie on the bag and stalked off, likely to deposit the winnings safely in his room.

"What are you going to spend yours on?" Velia asked, nodding to the money in Ferox's hand. "You could do with some nice pillows. Maybe a wall hanging? Or some new lamps? We could go shopping!" She grinned.

"Waste of money," he said curtly. "I won't be here long enough to enjoy such trifles."

Velia flinched, both at his tone and at the reminder he'd be gone as soon as the games finished. "You can take things with you, you know."

"No." His voice was gruff, the word final. "Too much hassle."

Velia folded her arms across her chest. "Where are you even going, anyway?" This was the first time they'd discussed the future—or at least, his future.

"Hispania." He tossed the pouch of coin lightly in his hand, looking at it, not her.

"Oh." A pang went through her. She hadn't realized he meant to go so far. She thought maybe he'd find a place in Rome, or somewhere close. Maybe they could still see each other, still…

Ferox took a step past her. "Excuse me," he muttered. "I need to put this away."

She watched him go, trying to pull her mind from such wistful thoughts as what might happen if he stayed in Rome. For a moment, she'd allowed herself to forget he'd be gone in a month, to fantasize about foolish things like redecorating his room.

She couldn't make that mistake again.

Ferox watched Velia from across the training ground as he permitted Achilles a brief break. They'd spent the afternoon drilling in hand-to-hand combat. Often, a fight would end with grappling in the sand until one man yielded, so it was important that Achilles develop his skills.

Velia was speaking with another man, someone Ferox didn't recognize. Guilt pinched him as he looked at her. He'd been rude earlier, he knew that, but he hadn't been able to stomach talking about the future with her.

He should find a way to apologize to her. Maybe he'd take her advice and buy a new pillow or two. It wouldn't cost much, and if it pleased her, it would be worth it.

His gaze moved from Velia to the man she was speaking with. There was something about the stranger he didn't like, though they were only talking. Velia was her usual smiling, chatty self. She gestured to the building behind her, which housed the kitchens and the dining space, as if giving directions.

The man was standing much too close to her, in Ferox's opinion, and Ferox could see the covetous look in his eye even from here. The stranger had the build of a gladiator, with a burly middle and muscular arms and shoulders.

Ferox beckoned Achilles over. "Do you know that man?" Since Ferox had been absent from the ludus for so long, there were still unfamiliar faces here, and Achilles had more contact with the younger gladiators.

The novice, wiping sweat from his face, trudged over. He squinted where Ferox pointed. "Don't think so. Visiting some-one?"

Technically, the guard at the gate was supposed to keep out anyone who didn't belong here, but the rule was loosely ob-served, and Ferox sensed the guard would look the other way with proper inducement.

Ferox grunted. "Maybe."

Achilles raised his ginger eyebrows. "Are you going to go disembowel him for speaking to your girl?"

"She's not my girl," Ferox growled.

"Then what do you care?" Achilles shot back.

"I don't."

Achilles rolled his eyes. "Wouldn't know it from your face."

Ferox glowered at him. "Three laps. Now."

With a long-suffering sigh, Achilles ambled off, breaking into a shuffling jog when he reached the perimeter of the training ground.

"Faster!" Ferox barked, and the novice increased his pace to an unhurried but acceptable run.

Once he was sure Achilles would maintain the speed, Ferox glanced back at Velia.

Both she and the stranger had vanished.

Anxiety rippled through him. His head whipped around, scanning, but he didn't catch sight of either. Instinct shouted that something was wrong. Perhaps Velia had gone to her room, or to Lucullus's office—but where did that leave the man she'd been talking to?

Something was amiss for them both to disappear at the same time.

His instincts had kept him alive in the arena, and he'd long ago learned to trust them.

Leaving Achilles to his laps, Ferox crossed the expanse of the training ground to where Velia had been standing, near the wall of the kitchen building. Still no sign of her.

A flicker of movement caught his attention, a flutter of fabric from around the other side of the building, where it formed a narrow alley next to the outer wall of the ludus.

Ferox went that way, then stumbled to a halt as he rounded the corner. Shock seized him.

The stranger had Velia pressed up against the wall, his hands fumbling to raise her skirt. Velia was frozen, her eyes shut tight.

Cold rage pulsed through Ferox. He took a step forward.

The next thing he knew, the man was on the ground before him, clutching at a bloodied nose. Ferox kicked him in the stomach. The impact shoved the man a few feet across the dirt.

With the stranger no longer an immediate threat, Ferox turned to Velia. She'd opened her eyes, and her gaze passed uncomprehendingly from her vanquished attacker to Ferox.

"Velia?" He moved toward her. Dimly, he sensed fury coursing through him, but everything felt distant, unreal, as it sometimes did during a fight in the arena. "Are you all right?" He extended a hand, meaning to touch her shoulder, but snatched it back as he realized his hand was covered in the other man's blood.

"I—" She broke off as footsteps sounded behind Ferox.

He whirled around, but it was just Achilles.

The novice's gaze swept over the scene, from Velia to the man on the ground. The stranger was just beginning to struggle to his feet, but Achilles marched over and dealt him a vicious kick to the head that made the man collapse to the dirt, unmoving. "Piece of pig shit," Achilles snarled.

Ferox turned back to Velia, but she slipped past him, hastening away. "Velia?" he called.

She didn't look back.

He needed to go after her, but he would deal with this first. "Get him out of here," he said to Achilles, nodding at the limp body before them. Ferox would have done it himself, but he didn't trust himself not to snap the man's neck if he laid hands on him.

Achilles nodded and bent down, taking hold of the man under his armpits. He dragged the body toward the outer gate of the ludus.

"And have a word with the guard," Ferox called after him. "See that he understands he's not to let anyone else in who doesn't belong here, or he'll have me to answer to."

Achilles gave another nod, then disappeared around the corner.

Ferox set off after Velia—she must have gone to her room—but paused when he remembered the state of his hands, now grown sticky with the man's blood. He took a brief detour to the fountain in the corner of the ludus, piped with water from the aqueducts, and scrubbed his hands.

The activity gave him a moment to come back to himself, to feel the rage and horror that had been hovering at the edges of his awareness since he went looking for Velia. It had all happened so fast. One moment he'd been contemplating his guilt over how rudely he'd spoken to her, crafting a plan to apologize.

Next he'd been bludgeoning the man who attacked her.

His hands shook beneath the trickle of water. Despite his years of fighting, he'd rarely done violence out of rage. Being a gladiator was not about fury or hatred, but about training and skill, not to mention a hefty dose of luck.

But the wrath that flooded him at the sight of that man's hands on Velia, her frozen expression—it threatened to overpower him.

He drew in a deep breath as he rubbed the last of the blood from his fingers. If he was going to speak to Velia, he needed to be in a more temperate state of mind.

He wiped his damp hands on his tunic, then headed toward the barracks.

18

V ELIA'S DOOR WAS CLOSED when he reached it. Ferox knocked gently. "Velia? Are you all right?"

He could hear her within, footsteps moving as if she was pacing.

Something smashed, the sound of pottery breaking. He jerked his head away from the door in surprise.

"Go away!" she yelled.

"No." He laid his palm flat on the surface of the door. It would be the work of a moment to remove it from his path. The thorny emotions still surging through him urged him to break, to smash, to rip the door from its hinges—anything to get to her.

But a brute breaking her door down was not what Velia needed right now, so he forced himself to adopt a more measured approach. Maybe *he* wasn't even what she needed right now. This situation required delicacy, and delicacy was not exactly his strong suit. "Would you like me to find Penthesilea?" he asked. "Perhaps…a woman…"

Then again, Lea was one of the least delicate people he'd ever met.

The door was yanked open, revealing Velia's blotchy face. "No," she hissed. Her arm shot out, and she dragged him inside by the front of his tunic, slamming the door behind him. "Did anyone else see?" she demanded. "Besides you and Achilles?"

Ferox shook his head, slightly bewildered by her anger. He'd expected her to be distraught, scared—not furious.

The evidence of her fury lay in shards of pottery on the floor, the remnants of a green-glazed water jug.

"Swear you won't speak of this to anyone." She crossed her arms over her chest. "Make Achilles swear too."

"I'll swear it, but don't you think your uncle should know?" Ferox took a tentative step closer to her. "I would bet that—that man belonged to another ludus. Lucullus could see an appropriate punishment administered."

Velia shook her head. Her hair cascaded around her face, the braid fully disintegrated. "No." Her shoulders hunched, and she turned away from him. "No one can know."

"But...why?"

"Because it shouldn't have happened!" The dim light glimmered on a tear hovering at the corner of her eye.

His heart clenched at the sight of it. For a brief, powerful moment, he was gripped with regret at not ending that man's life. He'd been so focused on getting him away from Velia and then out of the ludus, he hadn't even stopped to consider if the man deserved to draw breath anymore.

"I know," he murmured. "That bastard never should have lain a hand on you."

"That's not what I meant." The tear spilled down her cheek, and she drew in an unsteady breath. "I-I didn't fight. I just stood there. I didn't even scream!"

The anguish in her voice cut him deep. "Velia, that man was a trained gladiator. There was no way you could have—"

"Lea taught me how to fight," she interrupted. "She taught me what to do if someone—did that. But…I just couldn't…" Her voice broke.

He reached for her, and she sagged into his arms, clutching at him. He drew her against his body, holding her as tight as he dared. The feel of her eased some of the tension inside him, reassuring him that she was still whole, and alive, and real. "There's a reason gladiators train every day," he murmured. "It doesn't matter if you know how to do something. When you face it for real, that knowledge flies out of your head unless you've practiced so much it's ingrained into your very soul."

"I should have fought," she mumbled against his chest. "I didn't even *try*."

"If you fought, he would have hurt you." Darkness unfurled in his chest at the thought of what violence might have befallen her.

"So I was just supposed to let it happen?" She pushed away from him, ripping herself from his embrace. "You know very well what would have happened if you hadn't intervened at just that moment."

He had been trying not to think about it, but her words brought the sickening prospect to the front of his mind. "I know." There was no good answer, no rebuttal to what she said.

She hugged her arms around herself. "I shouldn't even be upset," she muttered. "I know far worse happens to women in this city every day, every night. I should be grateful." She glanced up at him. "How did you find us, anyway?"

At least this was a question he could answer. "I was watching you," he admitted. "I noticed when you disappeared."

"You were watching me?" She seemed bemused by the concept.

"Velia, whenever you're within sight of me, you're all I can think about."

"Oh," she murmured.

Ferox wasn't sure what to say next, so he turned his attention to the shattered jug. He gathered together the shards and piled them on the small table, bending to pluck the tiniest fragments from the floor. He didn't want her to step on one and injure herself.

She would need a new jug. He could buy her one. That would be an excellent use of his money, though replacing the pitcher would not undo the harm that had been done. Even so, the practical goal soothed him. He'd ask Jason to accompany him tomorrow if they had time. Ferox had no taste for decorative objects, as his hideous selection of rugs proved, but Jason understood these things better.

"You don't have to do that," Velia said as he swept the last bits of clay pieces into his palm and deposited them on the table.

"I don't mind." He dusted his hands clean.

She surveyed him uncertainly. "I...I know you should get back to Achilles, but..." Her fingers twisted at a curl of hair. "Would you stay? For a little while?"

He hadn't planned to leave her unless she demanded solitude, but her hesitant question made bittersweet warmth swell within him. "I'm not going anywhere. Achilles can take care of himself for an afternoon."

"Thank you." She passed a hand over her face with a long sigh. "Maybe it would be better if I kept busy, but I'm just…so tired."

He often felt that way after a fight, a bone-deep weariness that seemed to exceed any level of physical exertion. "Come here." He drew her over to her bed and sat down, pulling her into his lap. His arms wrapped around her, and she pressed her face to his shoulder.

She sniffled, and he realized she was crying again. These tears seemed different from the angry, frustrated tears of earlier. These seemed more like a release.

He had no idea how to comfort a crying woman—or a crying anyone, for that matter—but he settled for running his hand up and down her spine in what he hoped was a soothing motion. Maybe he should say something, but he doubted there was anything he could say that would make her feel better.

The shoulder of his tunic grew damp, but eventually she stilled and her breathing calmed. He pressed a kiss to the top of her head.

She slid off his lap and came to lie down, head pillowed on his thigh. He stroked her hair, fingers running through the wayward curls.

"Why Hispania?" she murmured after a while.

The question took him aback. As much as he didn't wish to discuss the future, he recognized that some distraction might benefit her. "I grew up there."

"Really?" She rolled onto her back, her head still atop his leg, and cast him a surprised glance. "*That's* where your accent is from."

"I don't have an accent." He'd grown up speaking both Latin and his native Cantabrian.

"Yes, you do. Just a little."

He let out a dissatisfied grunt, but decided to let her think she'd won.

"What name were you born with?" she asked.

It took him a moment to summon the long-disused word. "Larus." It felt strange on his tongue, like it belonged to someone he'd once known but hadn't thought of in years.

"How did you become…" She cleared her throat. "I mean, how did you end up in Rome?"

How did you become enslaved, he knew she meant. "I'm from the far north of the province. There was instability." The area he hailed from, Cantabria, had been the last region of Hispania to come under Roman control, and plenty still resented Roman rule. "A rebellion broke out. Those who weren't killed were enslaved."

"Oh." She stretched a hand up to brush his shoulder. "I'm sorry. Your family?"

"Dead." He alone had been the lucky one, young enough to be spared and sold into slavery. He'd been bought first by a gladiator trainer in the south of the province, in search of strong young men to train up. He'd changed hands a few times in the following years until ending up in Lucullus's service in Rome.

The wound of his parents' deaths, the loss of his home and childhood, had long since scabbed over, but he'd always carry it with him. As his body bore the scars of his fighting career, so the hidden parts of him would always be marked with his past loss.

Velia made a sound of sympathy. "I can understand why you want to go back. But…" She hesitated, rolling onto her side. "You never told me why you left my uncle. You stayed in Rome then, didn't you?"

"I spent nearly every coin I had on securing my freedom. I thought I could earn the rest of the money I'd need. I didn't realize…how hard it would be." There was a certain naïveté in living as a gladiator. Everything was paid for—food, housing, clothing, medical care, even female company if one desired it. After leaving the ludus, he'd quickly realized that the money he earned from winning fights was vastly more than freedmen with few skills and little education could make.

"But why did you leave?" she asked. "If you didn't have enough money, why not stay and earn more?"

He focused on gently untangling a small knot that had arisen in her curly hair. He'd guessed this question was coming, but this was a vastly more unpleasant subject than his plan to return to Hispania. "There was…another gladiator. A friend. His name was Hector." A slight shiver ran through him when he spoke the name. Names had power, and he'd been avoiding all mention of Hector's, hoping that would lessen the pull of his ghost. "He was killed in the arena."

If the loss of his home and parents was a long-healed scar, then Hector's slaying was a wound that festered, refusing to mend.

"I'm sorry," Velia whispered. Her hand slid over his knee in a soothing motion.

Ferox closed his eyes, but that only made the memories rise brighter in his mind, so he fixed his gaze instead on the strands of Velia's hair threading through his fingers, picking out all the various colors. Gold, wheat, sand, even a touch of ashy silver.

He knew he should end the conversation here, find a way to speak of something lighter. But words flew from his mouth like arrows from a bow, unable to be stopped. "It was my fault. He died because of me." The confession was ragged.

She half-sat up, turning to face him. "What?" Her eyes gleamed in the dim room. "Were you his opponent?"

He shook his head. "But I was supposed to be fighting that day. I was recovering from a minor injury, so he substituted for me. I could have still fought. The injury wasn't serious. If I'd just done what I was supposed to, he'd still be alive."

"But you might have died." She climbed back into his lap, her arms hooking around his shoulders. This time, he sensed it was for his comfort, not hers.

"Or I might have beaten the other fighter. We might both be alive today, if not for me backing out." His arms curled around her, pressing her close. Guilt overwhelmed him, stealing his breath for a painful moment. He didn't deserve her comfort, the warm pleasure of her in his arms. Hector had been robbed of all this, only because Ferox hadn't wanted to fight with a sprained ankle.

She burrowed her face against his shoulder. "I'm so sorry." She made no attempt to assuage his guilt, to tell him the fates had clearly ordained it this way and he should accept it. Instead, she just hugged him. "Will you tell me about him?"

The only thing that could induce him to speak of Hector was if it helped distract Velia. "He was from Germania. He spoke with a funny accent."

"Worse than yours?" A teasing lilt entered her voice.

"Given that I don't have an accent, yes, his was worse than mine."

Velia snorted.

"He'd flatten anyone who called attention to it," Ferox continued. "That was the only thing that could rile him, really." Other memories, long buried, rose in his mind. "He was the luckiest person I've ever met at dice. People always accused him of cheating, but he never did. He loved globi. Always stuffed his face with them. He became an expert at sneaking them past Lucullus." A smile twitched at his lips as he remembered Hector's fondness for the fried cheesecake balls. "He even paid a baker to deliver them here at the crack of dawn, before anyone else was up."

Velia made a noise of appreciation. "He had good taste."

"Yes." Ferox was silent for a moment, extending his awareness to see if he could sense Hector's shade lingering, pulled close by their talk of him. But Ferox felt none of the dread, the crushing guilt that usually accompanied his thoughts of Hector. He only felt a bittersweet warmth at the memories of his friend's distinctive accent, his talent for games of luck, and his fondness for globi.

Perhaps the ghost couldn't find him in Velia's room, he decided. Or maybe Velia really was a talisman against it. One more reason to keep her close…as if he needed another.

19

IN THE NIGHT, VELIA lay beside Ferox. He was asleep on his side behind her, his arm curled over her middle. He'd been so solicitous all afternoon—everything from cleaning up the vase she'd shattered to gently bullying her into eating something despite her lack of appetite.

He'd also confided in her about his lost friend. Her heart still ached at the pain and guilt that had been raw in his voice. Now she understood why he'd required such convincing to return to the ludus, and why he was so determined to leave. This place must hold many painful memories for him.

Tonight, Velia had her own shadows to deal with. Every time she dozed off, she'd jerk awake, haunted by a flash of memory from earlier. Her mind kept running over and over the interaction with that man, trying to identify any clues she'd missed, warnings she should have heeded.

The stranger had seemed nice enough at first. He was looking for someone, and she'd been happy to give him directions. She'd noticed him leering at her, but plenty of men leered without ever doing anything further.

"How much do you charge?" he'd asked. "You're a lupa, aren't you?"

She'd been only mildly offended that he mistook her for a prostitute. If a woman was seen inside the walls of the ludus, she must be a slave, prostitute, or gladiator. "I'm not, actually."

She'd turned to leave, but his hand closed around her upper arm.

"Well, if it's free…"

Before she could react, he'd dragged her around the corner of the nearest building, into the narrow alley behind.

She knew she should fight, scream, kick—but her body was frozen, pinned between the man and the wall behind her.

Then suddenly the man appeared at her feet, blood all over his face. Ferox was there, and moments later, Achilles.

Now, hours later, her body didn't seem to understand that she'd been saved. She could still feel the rough brickwork scraping her back through her dress, and her heart was still pounding.

She knew this brief, interrupted incident was nothing compared to what plenty of other women endured. Women who happened to go down the wrong street, or stay out an hour too late, or catch the eye of the wrong man. Or even be married to the wrong one.

Yet again, her mind went back to the moment before Ferox had intervened. In her imaginings, the incident played out as if he'd never arrived. She could feel the man's hands on her skin, grasping, bruising. A shudder went through her.

Velia extricated herself from beneath Ferox's arm, which, though limp with sleep, still felt as heavy as if it were made of concrete. She rose from the bed and paced her tiny bedroom.

She couldn't escape the horrible possibility of what would have happened if Ferox hadn't come, if he hadn't noticed her disappear, if he'd arrived a few moments later. The dark specter choked her, stoppering her breath. Her stomach turned, and she pressed a hand to the bare wall, hoping its cool solidity would steady her.

It didn't help.

Her mind was like a runaway cart, tumbling and crashing. She imagined the stranger overpowering her, forcing himself inside her, the tearing pain of violation.

What would her parents say if they knew about this? She could hear them clear as the sound of her own ragged breath. *Only what you deserve,* her father would spit. Her mother would nod. *Act like a whore, get treated like one.*

A sob escaped her lips.

Behind her, Ferox stirred. "Velia?" he mumbled. She heard his hands sweeping over the bed as if searching for her. "Velia?" he said again, his voice taking on a more urgent tone.

She found her voice. "I'm here."

He rose from the bed, a hulking shadow in the dark. "Are you all right?"

"Yes," she said reflexively, but her voice trembled. "No," she admitted.

His arms found her, clasping her shoulders. A hand slid up to caress her cheek.

She leaned into his touch, closing her eyes. "I keep thinking…about what would have happened if you hadn't been there. Hadn't stopped it."

He was silent for a moment. Then he spoke, his voice low and gravelly. "I would sell my soul to Dis if it would buy you a moment of peace from such thoughts."

The raw devotion in his voice took her breath away. *Dangerous*, she chided herself. *You're not supposed to be getting closer to him. Not when he'll be gone before you know it.*

But tonight, she didn't care if Ferox was leaving in a day or a week or a month. She needed his steady comfort, his unwavering presence.

She wrapped her arms around him, and he returned the embrace, leaning his head down to press against her shoulder. His touch soothed her, erasing the thoughts running rampant through her mind. This was what she needed—a touch that was pleasurable instead of unwanted, someone she could trust with her body and her soul.

"What if there was something else you could do?" she asked. "At not so high a price."

"Name it."

She ran her hands over his shoulders, taking comfort in their warm solidity. "I can't stop thinking about what might have happened. My mind just makes it worse and worse. I'm sure that doesn't make any sense. I know I should be grateful."

His fingers trailed over her back. "It doesn't need to make sense."

She tilted her head up to look at him, unable to make out much of his face in the midnight gloom. "I need you to make me forget. I want to replace my imaginings about what might have happened with something that *did* happen. But something good. Something I want. Do you understand?"

He said nothing for a moment. "Are you asking me to lie with you?"

"Yes," she breathed. She moved backward, drawing him with her, until her back made contact with the wall. "Like this." It was markedly similar to how she'd been with that man, pressed against a wall, unable to escape.

He hung back, putting a careful distance between them. "You really think that will help? It might distress you."

"Then we'll stop." In the darkness, she found his hands and placed them on her waist. "You said you'd sell your soul to make me feel better," she murmured. "I'm asking for something far…smaller." She put a teasing note into her voice as she slid her hand over his decidedly *not* small member. He stiffened at her touch, even through the fabric of his tunic.

"Velia…" Desire warred with hesitance in his voice.

"It's not so different from what you seek the night before your fights," Velia said. "Coupling distracts you, doesn't it? It soothes you. That's what I want."

His touch was the only thing that could wipe her mind clean of what had happened, that could truly bring her back to the here and now.

She hooked her leg around his, pressing their bodies even closer. For a moment, the closeness sent her straight back to the incident that afternoon, the panicked sensation of being pinned and helpless.

Ferox slid his hands up her sides, and the reverence in his touch returned her to the present. He lowered his head to brush her forehead with a kiss. "All right," he said. "But if we're going to do this, we're going to do it my way."

Before she could react, he was on his knees before her, gathering her skirt and lifting the fistfuls of fabric to her waist. "Hold this." He grasped her leg and hooked it over his shoulder, opening her to him. Then, his mouth was on her.

"Oh!" Her hands clenched around the bundle of linen as sensation exploded between her legs. She quaked, and his hand found her hip, holding her steady.

He worked her with his mouth, sucking and tonguing and nibbling, until she was panting, writhing between his head and the wall. He slid one finger inside her, then another, and the fullness drove her even higher.

Yes, this was what she needed—a pleasure so strong it chased away every thought, every fear, everything but this present moment.

Ferox released her hip and lowered his hand to his lap. The whispery sound that followed made her realize he was stroking himself, and a shudder ran through her. His groan vibrated against her. The thought of his hand working his cock as he pleasured her with his mouth was too much to bear.

Her fingers sought his head, gripping his skull to hold him close as she shattered against his mouth. A cry burst from her lips as her body bowed and quivered.

"Yes," he hissed, his fingers thrusting inside her. "More, Velia. Give me more."

She wrung every bit of pleasure from him that she could, then fell back, gasping. He gently withdrew his fingers from her and rose to his feet. His arousal bumped her, and she reached for it, fumbling his tunic over his head to bare his body, though she couldn't see much in the dark.

He made a low noise of need when her fingers slipped in the wetness dewing the head of his cock. "You still want this?"

"Yes. Now." He had satisfied her physically, but she wanted more. She wanted all of him, everything he could give her. His ardor, his touch, his devotion—they would burn away the shadows of earlier.

She wasn't entirely sure how the logistics would work, given the differences in their heights—but Ferox quickly solved that by lifting her off the floor. Her legs wrapped around his waist, and the pressure of his body held her against the wall.

"It feels wrong to want you like this," he whispered, "but I can't help myself."

His words made dark pleasure bloom inside her. She tightened the clasp of her legs around him. "Take me."

With a few adjustments of position, he rooted himself inside her. His hands grasped her bottom, effortlessly holding her up.

He let out a sharp sigh as she settled onto him. "Are you comfortable?"

She nodded. She was more than comfortable—she was swathed in blissful pleasure, enveloped in sensual delight. "But will you be able to hold me like this?"

He gave a raspy chuckle. "You weigh about as much as a feather pillow, and this won't take long at all. Trust me."

Velia giggled—and the noise quickly turned to a moan as he began to thrust. She could feel his need in the sharpness of each movement, but even so, she could tell he was holding back, setting a restrained rhythm.

She didn't want his restraint, his control. She wanted him to lose himself inside her, as he'd just made her lose herself. "Harder," she urged. "Faster."

"You're going to kill me," he grunted, but obliged, setting a relentless pace that had her body jumping up the wall with every thrust.

She grasped his muscled shoulders and held on. "Well, you did offer me your soul, didn't you?"

His movements became rougher. His fingers sank even harder into the flesh of her bottom, holding her tight to him.

She sensed he was getting close, and renewed the clasp of her legs around his hips. "I want you to spill inside me," she murmured in his ear.

"No," he groaned. "Don't say that."

"I have my herbs."

"Still—too—risky," he panted.

"But I want it," she wheedled. "Think of how good it will—*mmph!*"

His hand found her mouth, fingers gently but firmly muffling her words. "You can't talk if you're going to say things like that." His voice was unsteady, breathless as he drove into her, again and again, somehow still supporting her body with one arm.

She nipped him with her teeth. He grunted, but didn't release his hand. She bit him harder, sinking her teeth into his finger.

"Fuck," he hissed. A shudder wracked him, and he abruptly tore his hand from her mouth, pulling out of her as he exploded over the inside of her thigh. His hand grasped his cock, stroking hard and fast. He leaned his forehead against the wall with a deep groan.

Well. He'd foiled her plan to make him spill inside her, but she was fairly sure he'd just climaxed from her biting him. She tucked that piece of information away for further exploration.

Breathing hard, he helped her find her feet. Her legs wavered as soon as her feet touched the ground, and he slid an arm around her back to steady her.

Despite her body's instability, her mind felt, for the first time in hours, calm. She'd been right to ask this of him. It had shaken her loose from the twisting anxieties that gripped her, had brought her back to herself.

She fetched a cloth from her chest of drawers, which she used to clean both of them. Then, they stumbled together to the bed, collapsed onto it, and finally, Velia fell asleep.

20

FEROX WATCHED AS JASON lifted a large decorated jug and inspected it from all angles.

"Careful," the shopkeeper snapped. "You break it, you buy it." The man cast a suspicious glance at Ferox, who'd already had a near miss with a vase placed too close to the door. Only his quick reflexes had saved it from toppling to the ground.

Jason ignored the man's warning. "This is beautiful work," he murmured.

Ferox exhaled in relief. *Finally.*

During their break for the midday meal, Ferox had taken Jason to shop for a new pitcher for Velia. The errand had excited Jason, though he'd been critical about Ferox's choice of gift.

"Ladies usually prefer jewels, in my experience," Jason had said as they left the ludus. "And you certainly have the coin to get her something nice. Sapphires, maybe? They'd look good with her complexion."

"It has to be a pitcher."

"Why?"

"Hers broke." Ferox did not divulge the circumstances through which the jug had shattered. Thinking of yesterday still made rage heat his skin. Thankfully, this morning Velia had seemed closer to her normal cheerful self, and Ferox hoped she'd soon be able to put the incident behind her.

Jason let out a dissatisfied grunt. "If you insist."

They'd already visited two shops but left empty-handed. Jason had offended both artisans by pointing out inconsistencies in the decoration and irregularities in the shaping of the pottery. Ferox couldn't see any of what Jason noticed, and he'd thought all the vessels presented to them looked perfectly fine, but Jason wouldn't let him touch a single one.

Finally, they seemed to have found something that met Jason's approval. His dark eyes glowed with delight as he surveyed the big, round jug on the table before them. It depicted some sort of battle scene. The figures were molded onto the red surface of the jug in low-relief, each detail crisp and the surface polished to a bright gleam.

"This one is perfect," Jason pronounced. "Look at the composition! The details! The movement!" He turned to the shopkeeper. "We'll take it."

"Wait." Ferox held up a hand. "Jason, this is far too large. She won't be able to lift it when it's full." He suspected this piece was the sort of vessel meant for display, not usage, but Velia needed something practical.

Jason scowled.

The shopkeeper stepped forward. "It's for a lady? Perhaps you'd find this more fitting." He pointed behind them, and Ferox turned to see another jug resting on a shelf against the wall.

This one was a much more reasonable size, with an elegant curve to the body that tapered to a slender neck and flared spout. It featured intricate pattern work molded along the top and bottom. In the middle, three women danced, their dresses fluttering around them. Ferox leaned closer. The central woman carried a staff wrapped in ivy leaves and tipped with a pinecone—a thyrsus, borne by maenads during their worship of Bacchus.

Ferox didn't have Jason's artistic eye, but even he could appreciate the fineness of the work. The maenads' bodies were sensual and feminine, but they moved with a wild ferocity. The combination of beauty and fierceness reminded him of Velia. "I like it."

Jason inspected the pitcher, running a finger along the raised surface of the figures. Ferox held his breath, waiting for Jason to point out a flaw.

"It's beautiful," Jason finally admitted. "How much?"

Jason proceeded to engage in ruthless haggling with the shopkeeper, but the man would only agree to come down by fifty sestertii.

"Don't you know who that is?" Jason, exasperated, gesticulated at Ferox. "He's the emperor's favorite gladiator! Trust me, you want him to be talking up the beauty of your wares."

Ferox glared at Jason.

The shopkeeper cast a critical eye over Ferox. "Don't know. Don't care. Gaius Caesar himself could walk in here and I'd charge him the same."

Ferox pulled out the bag of money he'd brought. "The price is fair." He counted out the agreed-upon sum and handed the coins to the shopkeeper.

"Let me box this up for you." The man retreated to his back room for a moment, returning with a crate and a bundle of raw wool. He set the jug into the crate and carefully packed the wool around it. Then, he closed the crate and secured it with tightly wrapped cord.

Ferox thanked the man, tucked the box under his arm, and left the shop with Jason.

"We must have found the one person in the city who doesn't know who you are," Jason grumbled as they turned back toward the ludus.

Ferox gave a dry snort.

They walked in silence for the next block until Jason spoke again. "Is this a goodbye present?"

Ferox's steps faltered. He'd been doing an excellent job of blocking out all thoughts of the future, of the goodbyes that loomed larger with every passing day. "No," he grunted.

"If it's not a goodbye present, does that mean you're not leaving after the games are over?"

"I'm still leaving. The jug is just a present."

Jason shot him a sidelong glance. "So you're really going to go all the way to Hispania, all by yourself, leaving behind everyone who cares about you?"

"You'll all survive without me."

"Yes, but there's more to life than surviving," Jason argued.

"Even if I stayed, how long do I have left? Can't fight forever. Better to take the money and enjoy the rest of my life in peace. You should start thinking along the same lines. Lea too."

Jason shot Ferox a sidelong glance. "I don't know about Lea, but as for me, well, I prefer not to think past the current week. Or day, sometimes."

Ferox envied Jason's unworried attitude toward the future. But Jason didn't have to contend with the vengeful ghost of their friend. Ferox said nothing of Hector. Jason had clearly found some peace with the death, and this was Ferox's burden to bear, alone.

Jason clapped him on the back and increased his pace. "No matter what the jug is for, I'm eager for the verdict. If she likes it, then I picked it out. If she doesn't like it, then it was entirely your choice, understand?"

21

A KNOCK CAME AT Velia's door shortly after she entered her room, having just returned from the evening meal. When she answered it, she saw Ferox, and a pleased smile spread over her face. A crate was tucked under his arm, and he held it out to her as soon as she opened the door.

"For you," he said.

"Me?" She eyed the box with surprise as she brought it into her room. She laid the crate on the table and beckoned him inside. "What is this?"

"Open it."

She untied the cord binding the crate's top. Inside, something was covered with tufts of wool. She brushed them aside to reveal the flared spout of a jug. "Oh!" She pulled the object out, handling it with careful fingers.

She blinked at it, hardly able to absorb the intricacy of the sculpted figures that emerged from the gleaming red pottery. "What—why?" she managed, overcome.

He shrugged. "Yours broke. You needed a new one."

Her eyes stung as she beheld the stunning pitcher. It was the most beautiful thing she'd ever seen, let alone owned. If she wasn't mistaken, the scene depicted a group of three maenads, fervent and fierce in their worship of the wine god.

Ferox frowned. "If it's going to make you cry, I'm taking it back."

She clutched the jug to her chest. "No! It's—it's beautiful. It's just…no one's ever given me something like this." It must have cost a fortune. "It's too fine. I feel as if I shouldn't even be touching it." Despite her words, she traced a finger over the delicate figures, feeling the ridges and curves of the sculpted pottery.

"If you won't use it, then I'm also taking it back."

He made as if to grab for it, and she batted his hand away, giggling. "All right, I promise to use it!"

"You should know, Jason helped select it," Ferox said. "He made me promise to give him credit if you liked it."

"You went shopping with Jason?" The image of the two gladiators going shopping together for a pitcher—for *her*—was delightfully incredible.

"He has an eye for these things." Ferox waved a hand at the jug. "He was extremely picky. I'm assured it's of very fine quality."

"I can see that," she murmured, her eyes running over the perfect, expressive forms.

"So you like it?" he pressed.

She nodded. "I love"—*you*—"it."

I love you. The words she'd only barely stopped herself from saying reverberated around her mind. She stared unseeingly at the vessel.

No, you idiot. You don't love him. You love his shoulders, his jawline. And his cock—definitely his cock. You love his hands, the way he holds you even in sleep. You love how he fixes your hair before you notice it's come undone. You love that he bought not one, not two, but three rugs.

*You love how he protects you, how cherished he makes you feel.
Oh no.*

She felt as if the jug were about to slip from her fingers, so she turned and set it safely on the table. Her hands shook, and more tears welled in her eyes. She kept her back to him for a moment, needing to master herself, needing to keep this feeling at bay.

She couldn't love him. He was going to leave, and it would break her heart.

His hands caressed her shoulders. "I really didn't mean to make you cry."

Velia scrubbed away the tears clinging to her eyelashes and turned to face him. "It's the most beautiful thing I've ever seen."

He slid a hand up to stroke her cheek, thumb slipping in a teardrop. "It's only the second most beautiful thing in this room." He bent his head and brushed her lips with his.

She deepened the kiss, twining her arms around his neck. *This* was something she understood—lust, hunger, need. She would try to forget her disconcerting realization, let him distract her with the pleasure they could find together. A good bedding could distract from anything, as she'd learned last night.

She pulled back from the kiss. "I have a question for you." She trailed a finger down his face, over his lips, watching his eyes darken with desire as she did. "Why didn't you tell me you like being bitten?"

He jumped as if she'd pinched him. "I—what do you—I don't—" he stammered, cheeks reddening.

She raised her eyebrows. "Last night, I'm fairly certain you climaxed when I bit you. Didn't you?"

"I…maybe?" he confessed. "I don't know. No one's ever done that before. I didn't—I didn't expect it."

"I'd like to try it again," she murmured. Pushing gently on his chest, she walked him over to the bed, pausing to strip off his tunic. At the sight of his body, desire flared, throbbing and hot between her legs. His cock was already stiffening, but she paid it no mind…for now.

She laid him on the bed, then climbed atop him, straddling his broad torso. His hands came up to stroke her thighs, still covered by her dress. He gazed at her, wariness mingled with lust in his eyes.

"How does this feel, I wonder?" She leaned down and took hold of his earlobe with her teeth—just a light nibble.

He twitched beneath her, choking back a gasp.

His reaction pleased her. She moved down, grazing her teeth over his neck. She found the one spot she knew was the most sensitive and gave him a sharp but quick nip.

"Fuck, Velia," he groaned. "You'll be the death of me, I swear."

She laughed, a trifle smugly. "Imagine being a big, strong gladiator—the emperor's favorite, no less—conquered by a few little nibbles." She scooted down his body and took one of his nipples between her teeth.

He let out another deep groan. "You know you can bring me to my knees with barely a glance, Velia."

She liked the sound of that, though his devotion was dangerous. It intoxicated her, like unmixed wine. She'd lose herself in it if she wasn't careful.

She moved further down, littering his chest and stomach with alternating kisses and nips. He jumped at each one, the powerful muscles tensing and releasing beneath her.

He hissed as her hand found his cock. She gave him one stroke, and he shuddered at the pass of her hand. Then, she lowered her head to take him into her mouth. He grunted a curse.

She took him as deep as she could, and on the way back up, allowed her teeth to graze against him. His hand tangled in her hair, and he moaned, fingers tightening.

"Careful," she murmured as she released him from her mouth. "Or I'll have to tie you up again." She enjoyed his touch too much to do that, but it was rather fun to tease him.

Velia nipped the head of his cock lightly, and he jerked so hard he nearly threw her off him. She giggled, planting her weight more securely on his legs. She worked him with her mouth again, bringing him to the point where he was gasping, shuddering, writhing beneath her.

Then, she removed her mouth and replaced it with her hand. She nudged his muscular thighs apart and lowered her head to the surprisingly soft skin on the inside of his thigh. As her hand worked him, she brushed her lips over his skin once, a caress, then sank her teeth into the flesh of his thigh.

His hips bucked, and suddenly he was exploding over her hand. She bit him again, just for good measure. His hand shot down to grasp hers, holding her fingers tight around him as the climax tore through him.

When he finally slumped back onto the bed, chest heaving, she surveyed her handiwork. Her teeth left two red semi-circles on the inside of his thigh. They would fade soon, but for the time being, she liked that he was marked by her.

He was hers, at least for a little while longer.

She cleaned his seed off her hand and his cock, but when she made to lie next to him, he shook his head. "Not done with you yet." His voice was still breathless, slurred.

He patted the spot on the mattress next to his head. A smile grew on her lips as she realized what he wanted. She climbed up his body, sinking her quim down onto his face. A moan escaped her lips as his tongue found her. She was throbbing and slick, her desire inflamed by the pleasure of tormenting him as she had.

Velia flattened her hands against the wall and arched her back to settle her hips more fully onto him. She felt him groan against her, and his hands slid over her thighs, holding her tight.

His lips clasped around her most sensitive spot. A tremor shot through her, the pleasure sharp and tingling. "Right there," she panted. "Just like that." Her hips flexed, moving in rhythm with the suction of his mouth. She rode his face, taking everything he gave her.

The pleasure coiled tighter and tighter inside her. One hand slipped from the wall to find his head, fingers anchoring in his hair. Her eyes fluttered shut, blocking out everything but the feel of him beneath her, the soft yet demanding way he worked her with his mouth. She chased the pleasure with every twitch of her hips, every quiver of her thighs.

Finally, it crashed over her, consuming her in blissful spasms that felt endless. She moaned, the noise raw and frenzied. His fingers dug harder into her thighs as she writhed atop him.

"Enough," she gasped as the shudders faded. She lifted herself off him, thighs trembling. Somehow, she found her way to collapse beside him. He wiped a hand across his mouth, then kissed her forehead.

As she settled against him, her gaze lit on the new pitcher on the other side of the room. Bittersweet emotion welled in her chest. How was she supposed to say goodbye to all of this? Her eyes stung, and she hid her face against his shoulder. She released a long, unsteady breath.

"Velia?" His fingers traced through her hair. "Are you all right?"

She smoothed a hand over his chest and strove to steady her voice. "Just tired."

He curled his arm around her shoulders. "Sleep," he murmured. "I'll be here when you wake."

22

THE NOISE OF THE crowd roared in Ferox's ears as he made his way to the center of the arena. The announcer gesticulated, coaxing the crowd's fervor to new heights even though only the privileged few could hear him.

This was Ferox's second of three fights, which meant he was halfway through his allotted time at the games.

Halfway through his time with Velia.

The past two weeks had been a blur of days spent sweating in the sun barking at Achilles, and nights entangled with Velia. She'd been aggressive in booking Achilles for three more matches. It was unusual for a gladiator to fight that often, but these games were quite possibly a once-in-a-lifetime opportunity for a novice to make a reputation for himself, and Velia was determined to take advantage of it. Ferox admired her doggedness, the unyielding way she pursued what she wanted.

Her strategy was working, for Achilles had won each of those three fights. Each time he fought, the crowd cheered louder. Velia had even suggested that he forego his helmet, allowing his red hair to become his signature symbol in the arena. Fighting without a helmet represented a foolish degree of bravado in Ferox's opinion, but Achilles soaked up the attention. The novice was quickly becoming a rising star, and he grew more cocky with each win.

While Achilles's triple victories swelled his ego, they also bolstered his discipline and effort at training. Like any gladiator, he was becoming intoxicated by the thrill of winning, not to mention the monetary prizes he gained. Many mornings, when Ferox finally pulled himself out of bed with Velia, he found Achilles already on the training ground, running laps to warm up or bludgeoning a boxing bag with his fists.

Achilles had even—just once—beaten Ferox in a practice match. It was really Velia's fault. She'd been leaning against a column to watch them fight, and a breeze had whipped up, briefly lifting the hem of her dress. The flash of creamy thigh had been enough to distract Ferox, and Achilles seized the advantage.

Velia had cackled and teased him for a solid day after that.

Thankfully, today she was out of his line of sight, watching from the shadows with her uncle.

Ferox's gaze snapped to his opponent, who entered on the other side of the arena. The man fought in the style of a retiarius: he carried no sword or shield, but bore a weighted net in one hand, a trident in the other. A dagger hung at his hip for close combat. Lightly armored, he wore no helmet.

Ferox assessed him as they drew closer to each other. They were matched in height, and the man moved with a long, easy stride. His wrist flicked the net out in front of him in a practiced movement.

As they took up positions opposite each other at the official's direction, Ferox finally looked at the man's face.

A jolt went through him. For a brief, dizzying moment, it felt as if the sand were falling away beneath his feet.

It was the very man he'd pulled off Velia two weeks ago.

"You," he snarled as the official gave the signal for the match to begin. They circled each other, Ferox staying out of reach of the net as it whispered over the sand. The greatest danger in fighting a retiarius was how the net kept an opponent at just the right distance for the long trident to strike.

The man's eyebrows shot up, perhaps recognizing Ferox despite his helmet. "Ah, I thought that might have been you." His tone was relaxed, almost jovial. "Listen, I owe you an apology. I never would have laid a hand on the whore if I'd known she was yours."

"She's not a whore," Ferox growled. *But she is mine.*

"It was an honest mistake," the man continued, sounding for all the world as if he were apologizing for stepping on Ferox's toe in a crowded tavern. "You can't blame me. It's not like she put up much of a fight."

Rage engulfed Ferox like a spark catching dry tinder. He struggled to tamp it down. Rage had no place in the arena. Winning fights was about skill, training, and strategy. It was not about giving into the violent emotions that currently pulsed through him.

As Ferox was striving to convince himself not to leap for the man's throat then and there, his opponent jabbed out with the trident in a lightning-fast strike. Ferox leaped back, but not quickly enough. The triple points of the trident sank into the muscle of his thigh, just below the edge of his shield.

Pain seared. The crowd gasped.

Ferox made a split-second decision based on two factors. First, he immediately knew this wound was bad. Even if it didn't kill him, it would weaken him sooner rather than later, so he needed to end this fight before his strength failed. Second, his opponent would expect him to fall back after such a wound, to take a breath and assess the injury.

So Ferox did the opposite. He tossed aside both his sword and heavy shield, then leaped at the man, heedless of how his feet tangled in the net. A retiarius always expected his opponent to avoid the net at all costs, but the net no longer mattered if they were both tangled in it. Which was exactly what happened as Ferox slammed into the man, taking them both down to the sand.

At this close range, the trident was useless, and Ferox easily wrenched it from the man's grip. They scuffled, sand flying. Ferox's main goal was to keep his opponent's hands occupied so he couldn't go for the dagger at his waist.

The man managed to flip Ferox onto his back, hands seeking his throat, but Ferox kneed him in the stomach and reversed their positions. A blow hit his jaw, and he tasted blood. The scorching pain in his thigh spread over his entire leg, and he could feel the limb becoming slippery as it bled. Weakness would set in soon, and then his chance at victory would disappear.

And he would *not* lose to this man.

He summoned one last burst of strength. Finally, he got his hands around the other man's throat. He squeezed ruthlessly.

The man clawed at his grip for a moment, then fluttered a hand into the air. "Yield," he croaked. "I yield."

Ferox had forgotten that yielding was an option. He wanted to keep squeezing, to feel the man's neck crack and collapse beneath his fingers, to watch the life fade from his frantic eyes.

But Ferox forced himself to relinquish his grip. The man rolled onto his side, gasping for breath.

Ferox struggled to his feet, disentangling himself from the net. His wounded leg nearly gave out, but he managed to stand. He grabbed his nearby sword and pointed it at the throat of his opponent, who had now dragged himself to a kneeling position.

Ferox's eyes fixed on the emperor, who would decide the fate of this man. Ferox had never actually wanted to kill one of his opponents before, but this time, he found himself praying for the thumb-out gesture that would signal death.

Let me kill him, Ferox silently urged the emperor. Rage still coursed through him in white-hot waves, and he wanted nothing more than to sink his sword into the man's neck.

The shouts from the crowd were mixed, but they seemed to trend toward mercy. The emperor leaned against the balustrade of his viewing area, considering. Then he held out a hand.

A closed fist. Mercy.

Ferox shut his eyes.

No. Mercy was no longer an option.

He opened his eyes and drew the sword across the man's throat in a slow, deliberate motion. Blood spurted from the thin slice. The man clapped a hand to the wound, gaze flicking up to Ferox in shock.

The crowd went silent. So silent Ferox could hear his own blood pounding in his ears.

The man slumped to the sand, and Ferox watched the life leave his eyes with primal satisfaction.

Amid the crowd's still-shocked silence, he trudged from the arena, one thought resounding in his mind: *better late than never.*

23

Lucullus accosted Ferox as soon as he stepped off the arena's sand. "What *the fuck* have you done?" he demanded.

Behind Lucullus, Velia stood, white-faced and frozen, a hand pressed to her mouth.

Ferox pushed past Lucullus. "I killed him." He could deal with Lucullus later. Right now, his chief concern was finding somewhere to sit before his leg gave out on him.

"I know that," Lucullus growled. "Twenty thousand people know that! What I want to know is *why*. Did you go blind? Why, by all the shades of the underworld, would you disregard the decision of the *fucking emperor*?"

"He deserved it." Ferox limped through the passage into the wider space where the other gladiators waited for their own fights. News must have already filtered through, for everyone was staring at him. Lea, off to the side, caught his eye and gave him a slow, approving nod.

As far as Ferox was concerned, that man had forfeited his life as soon as he laid a hand on Velia against her will. The cretin had lived two weeks longer than he should have, but at least now Ferox had rectified his lapse.

Ferox found a stool against the wall and sank down onto it, suppressing a hiss of pain. No sooner had he sat than the ludus's physician appeared at his side. The man made critical noises as he examined the wound.

Lucullus followed Ferox and hovered at his other side, fists clenched. Ferox had never seen the man so angry. Usually, when something displeased the manager, he reacted with cold disappointment. But now, he looked as if he were about to combust with rage. "I need a better reason than that," Lucullus snarled.

The physician cleaned Ferox's wound with about as much gentleness as if he were scrubbing a floor. Ferox gritted his teeth.

Velia trailed behind her uncle. "Uncle, please. He's wounded. Surely you can speak once he's rested."

Lucullus shot her a sharp sidelong look. "Seeing as he's currently receiving medical care *I* pay for, he can talk now."

"You don't understand," Velia insisted, her voice trembling. "This was all my fault."

Lucullus whirled around to face her. "You? What could you possibly have to do with this?"

"Velia," Ferox warned as she opened her mouth to speak. Everyone was still staring at them—far too many eyes and ears. Ferox knew she didn't want anyone to know about the incident, and he wouldn't let her speak of it here.

Velia met his gaze. "Tell him."

Ferox jerked as the physician drove a threaded needle into his skin. It had been a long time since he'd had a wound that required stitching, and he'd forgotten how damned painful it was. "Not here," he ground out. Lucullus would need to know the truth, but it could be shared in private. "We will speak in your office at the ludus."

Lucullus glowered at him. "You'll come straight there as soon as you've been stitched up. I don't care if you have to be carried in."

"Fine," Ferox grunted.

Lucullus stormed off. Velia cast Ferox one distraught look, her gaze flicking anxiously from his face to the bloody mess on his leg, then hurried after her uncle.

"How bad is it?" Ferox asked the physician, whose head was bent over the wound as he worked.

The man shrugged. "Could have been worse. A little to the left and you'd be dead already." He made another agonizing stitch. "You'll probably take ill with a fever for a few days. Which will be for the best, since you'll need to stay off that leg for a while."

"Very well." Ferox closed his eyes while the physician finished his work.

"You should rest here before returning to the ludus," the physician advised as he snipped the final thread.

Ferox hauled himself to his feet. "I need to get back." He felt somewhat steadier after the brief respite, but his leg still burned with pain. The prospect of walking even the short distance to the ludus was deeply unpleasant, but he had no choice.

Jason materialized next to him, looping an arm under his shoulders. Ferox glanced at him in surprise. "Where did you come from?" Jason wasn't due to fight today, so he'd remained behind at the ludus.

"Lea fetched me." Jason supported Ferox as they slowly proceeded to the arena's back exit.

Ferox felt a rush of gratitude. Lea must have jogged to the ludus, found Jason, and returned with him.

"I don't suppose you'll tell me what happened?" Jason asked as they walked—or hobbled in Ferox's case—through the streets. Thankfully, the streets were empty, everyone else still at the games, so no one was around to gawk.

"No."

"Lea has a theory." Jason adjusted his grip on Ferox's shoulders. "The only reason you'd kill like that is in retaliation for harming someone you care about. Nothing's happened to me or her, so that leaves…Velia."

"Lea is very perceptive," Ferox grunted.

They traveled the rest of the way to the ludus in silence.

Lucullus awaited them in his office. Velia stood beside his desk, fingers twisting anxiously. Jason deposited Ferox in the spare chair, then left with a nod to the other two.

Ferox felt light-headed with pain, but he strove to block it all out and assume a relaxed posture in the chair. Velia was eyeing him with concern, and he didn't wish to cause her any more distress.

Lucullus's fiery rage seemed to have cooled, and his usual composure was back. But frustration still simmered in his gray eyes. "Explain," was all he said after Jason shut the door behind himself.

Ferox glanced at Velia in silence. It was, after all, her story to tell.

Velia met his gaze. "It was my fault, as I said earlier," she said in a small voice.

"No, it wasn't," Ferox growled.

She ignored him. Her hands smoothed over and over her braid where it hung across her shoulder. "That man—he came to the ludus a few weeks ago. He—he—" She swallowed hard. Her cheeks flushed, and she stared at the floor. "Just tell him," she pleaded.

Ferox shifted in the chair, fruitlessly trying to find a more comfortable position for his leg. "I killed that man because he disrespected Velia. Laid hands on her. I should have done it sooner."

Lucullus narrowed his eyes, gaze flicking from Ferox to Velia. "Is this true?" he demanded of his niece.

Velia nodded.

"Did he violate you?"

The color in her cheeks deepened. "Ferox intervened before it got that far."

Lucullus let out a long breath. Ferox couldn't tell what the man was thinking, and his hands curled around the arms of the chair. If Lucullus dared utter a single word that made Velia feel ashamed of what happened to her...

The manager rose from behind his desk and came to stand before Velia. He rested a hand on her shoulder. "My dear," he murmured. "Why didn't you tell me? I could have seen justice done."

Ferox relaxed. Usually, Lucullus and Velia treated each other with the brisk respect of employer and employee. Aside from the fact that they shared a diminutive stature, he might have never known they were related if he hadn't been told. This was the first time Ferox had detected any sort of familial warmth between them.

"I-I don't know," Velia admitted. "I was embarrassed."

Lucullus patted her shoulder. "I see. Now that I understand the situation, you may go. I'd like to speak with Ferox alone."

Velia nodded. She cast one more glance at Ferox, her eyes lingering on his wounded leg, then slipped from the room.

Lucullus returned to his seat behind his desk, the fingers of one hand gently drumming the wooden surface. "There will be ramifications from this. One does not disregard the orders of the emperor without consequence."

Ferox nodded, though in truth he hadn't been thinking that far ahead when he drew his sword across that man's throat.

"I hope it does not need to be said that you'll forfeit any winnings you might have received. And then there is the matter of the fee for the dead man." When a gladiator was slain, the host of the games had to pay a high price—often several times what the gladiator himself was worth—to the dead fighter's manager.

While the emperor himself was the host of the games, Ferox supposed it made sense the ruler couldn't be expected to outlay the cost for a man he'd intended to spare. "Take it out of my earnings."

Lucullus nodded. "The emperor's man already paid me half the fee for your second appearance. I imagine that will all go toward payment for the dead man. But the cost may be higher."

Ferox's jaw tensed. This was dearly cutting into the money that was supposed to buy him a new life. "Take it out of my next fee, then."

"That's assuming you have a next appearance. The emperor would be well within his rights to expel you from the games after the stunt you pulled."

A burst of shock pulsed through Ferox, momentarily overtaking the pain in his leg. Surely not. Surely the emperor wouldn't go so far as to remove him from the games.

If that happened, he'd not only lose his chance at earning the rest of his promised money, but he'd also lose his last weeks with Velia.

"You don't think…Would he do that?" Ferox demanded.

Lucullus shrugged. "Far be it from me to anticipate the workings of an emperor's mind."

Ferox blinked stupidly as the potential consequences of his actions crashed over him. With one split second decision, he might have ruined everything.

Even so—he didn't regret it, not for a moment.

"The emperor has sisters, doesn't he?" Ferox asked with a touch of desperation. "Maybe—I could explain. Any man would have done the same—"

Lucullus shook his head. "No matter your reasoning, you still disrespected him in front of thousands of people. I advise you to pray to any god who will hear you that the rest of the games today are sufficiently entertaining to distract him from what you did." Lucullus surveyed Ferox with cool dispassion. "You and Velia are lovers, aren't you?"

Ferox should have known that question was coming. He struggled to meet Lucullus's steady gray gaze. "Yes," he admitted. "I know it was wrong of me to trifle with her." If Ferox took responsibility for their dalliance, he hoped to shield Velia from her uncle's displeasure.

Lucullus snorted. "If I know my niece, I highly doubt you had much choice in the matter. I only wanted to confirm what I've suspected for weeks."

"You—you knew?" Ferox couldn't imagine any man being tolerant of a woman under his protection consorting with a gladiator.

Lucullus lifted his gaze skyward. "I'm not her father—who, by all accounts, has abdicated any concern for her welfare. If I'd known your little entanglement would have led us here, I'd have put a stop to it, but it seems it's too late now." He let out a resigned sigh. "Now, you look ready to collapse. Get some rest. Jason!" He rapped an inkwell on his desk.

There was more Ferox wanted to say—how deeply he cherished Velia, how she was in his thoughts day and night, how a single smile from her could warm him all the way to his toes…but saying things like that would lead to questions he couldn't answer and promises he couldn't make.

The door opened, and Jason reappeared. Ferox should have known he'd be lurking outside, anticipating the need to help Ferox from the office.

Jason heaved Ferox to his feet, and together they stumbled out of the room.

Velia waited in his bedroom. In the time since she'd left the office, she'd procured a vat of steaming water and a stack of clean cloths. "Thank you," she murmured as Jason sat Ferox on the edge of the bed, leg stretched out on the floor.

"Do you need my help with anything?" Jason asked.

Velia shook her head, wetting a cloth in the warm water. "I can manage."

Jason nodded. "Try not to die," he advised Ferox, then left.

"Velia, you don't have to—" Ferox began, but Velia shushed him. She knelt next to his wounded leg and began to gently wash it. The physician had cleaned the area immediately around the wound, but the rest of his leg was still covered in sticky, drying blood.

Despite the pain, the softness of her touch soothed him, a healing magic no physician could provide.

He couldn't see her face from this angle, but her breath hitched, and her hand shook where it rubbed the damp cloth over his leg. A pang shot through him as he realized she was crying. He reached down to caress her cheek. "Velia?"

She pulled away from his touch with a sniffle. "This is all m-my fault. You could have died, and it would have been my fault!"

"Velia, you weren't in the arena. What happened in there was between me and him."

She shot him a watery glare. "You killed him for me."

And I'd do it again. "That doesn't mean it was your fault."

She shook her head. "If I hadn't been so *stupid*, none of this would have happened. My parents would say I deserved it. Act like a whore, get treated like one." She wrapped her arms around herself, and in that moment, his heart ached even worse than his leg.

"Your parents are lucky I don't know where they live," he said in a low voice.

"I don't often think they're right," she whispered. "But maybe this time...I-I was too nice to him. I smiled at him. Maybe if I'd been colder—"

"You've smiled at every man in the ludus and none of them has tried to attack you. And if they have, tell me and I'll end their lives this moment. Am I wrong?"

Velia wiped a hand across her eyes. "No," she admitted.

He leaned forward, ignoring the pain at the change of position, and ran a finger along the curve of her jaw, gently tilting her face to look at him. "What happened with that man had nothing to do with who you are or how much you smile. It had everything to do with who that man is. *Was*," Ferox corrected himself with a touch of dark satisfaction. "He saw someone smaller, weaker than himself and took advantage. As for your parents, well, they're hateful idiots. I don't know how they could have spent twenty years raising you and not thank the gods every day for blessing them with you. They don't deserve you."

She caught his hand and twined her fingers through it. He must have said something right, for some of the distress faded from her eyes. "I just...I can't stand seeing you hurt. When I saw him stab you, it felt like I'd been stabbed."

"Surely you've seen gladiators be wounded before."

"Yes, but not one I..." Her gaze flicked to his then slid away. She returned to gently scrubbing his leg clean of dried blood.

She didn't finish her sentence, but she didn't have to. A ball of warmth seemed to explode behind Ferox's ribs, chasing away all his pain for one sweet moment. He'd sensed this thing between them was growing into more than simple lust, and today proved it. Jason was right: Ferox would only kill for someone he cared about.

Someone he loved.

And if Velia possibly felt the same about him…that was both the best and worst thing he could imagine. Because if the emperor expelled Ferox from the games, he'd be parted from her.

Ferox closed his eyes. He couldn't dwell on that now, not with his body exhausted and wracked with pain. For now, all he could afford to think about was the pleasure of her touch and the fact that maybe, just maybe, she loved him too.

24

A S THE PHYSICIAN WARNED, the fever set in the next day. Ferox almost didn't mind it, as he was bedbound anyway and it addled his mind enough to distract from the pain.

But as the fever intensified over the following day and night, it brought vivid, unsettling dreams—or at least, what he hoped were dreams. Over and over again, he relived the moment he'd drawn his sword across his opponent's throat. But just as the blood began to spurt, Ferox glanced at the man's face, only to see it shift and blur into that of Hector. His friend clutched at his bleeding neck, slumping to the sand as the life drained from his body.

Other times, a squadron of red-garbed Praetorians, bristling with armor and weapons, burst into his room and dragged him from his bed. His leg left a bloody trail behind him. As the Praetorians hauled him through the streets, he looked up to find that each had Hector's face. And not the smiling, kind face he wanted to most remember. It was instead how Hector had appeared moments after death—bloodied, one eye a gaping hole, skull partially crushed.

When Ferox fought, the soldiers held him down. They shifted into the figures of Jason, Velia, and Lea. In his moments of clarity, he realized with relief that those three were the ones with him. Not the emperor's Praetorians, and not the mangled Hector.

Velia was always there, day and night. She fed him bites of food and sips of water, and cooled him with damp cloths that smelled of lavender. He tried to tell her to leave, that she needed to rest, but either he never succeeded in saying the words aloud or she simply ignored him.

Gradually, the moments of clarity lasted longer and longer. His fever eased, and finally, he woke in the middle of the night not to a terrifying dream, but to the darkened surroundings of his room and the quiet sound of Velia's breathing coming from somewhere on the floor.

Moving gingerly, he raised himself to a sitting position. His body felt weak—even the minimal effort of sitting up made his head spin—and his thigh ached, but the searing pain of the early injury had faded.

He squinted at the floor beside his bed. He could just make out Velia's small shape, curled up atop the rugs, a pillow beneath her head.

She stirred. "You're awake," she mumbled. Then she was on her feet, a cool hand pressed to his forehead. "You feel better. Let me get you some water."

"Velia." His voice was scratchy. He'd once swallowed a mouthful of sand in the arena, and that was exactly how his throat felt right now. "You shouldn't be here."

She held out a cup of water to him. "I think you mean, thank you *so* much for taking such good care of me while I almost died from a fever."

He flushed. Awake for barely a moment and he'd already said something stupid. "You're right. I'm sorry. Thank you." He took the water from her and drank deeply.

She rewarded him with a pass of her hand through his hair. He closed his eyes for a moment, luxuriating in the pleasure of her touch, but something less pleasant soon jumped into his mind.

"The…emperor," he said, voice still raspy despite the water. "Any word?"

Velia shook her head. "Nothing."

"How long has it been?"

"Nearly a week."

Ferox lay back against the wall. A week with no word, no order that Ferox be removed from the games. Could he really be that lucky? Had the emperor forgotten, or did he not care enough to punish Ferox for his defiance?

No, Ferox decided. Something was still coming. And when it did…

"We need to talk," he said.

"You should rest."

"I've been resting for a week." He held out a hand to her, and she approached the bed, perching on the edge. Her fingers twined with his. "Velia, if the emperor should force me to leave the games…I want you to come with me."

He couldn't see much of her expression in the darkness, but he felt her fingers tense. "What?"

He could sense her doubt, her uncertainty, but he pushed past it, laying out the plan that was hazily coming together in his mind. "I don't have as much money as I'd anticipated, but I still have more than I left here with the first time. Enough to make it to Hispania, buy a bit of land, build a little house. We could plant a field and keep animals. It may be difficult at first, but we can make a life for ourselves."

"Ferox…" Her voice wavered. "I can't…Achilles is here."

"Sign him over to your uncle," he urged.

She rose from the bed, pacing in the small room. "You're asking me to leave the ludus. Leave Rome. Go to Hispania with you. Are you asking me to *marry* you?" She spoke the sentence as if it were the most ludicrous thing she'd ever contemplated.

Ferox had not been thinking in such specific terms. All he wanted was her; he didn't much care about marriage. But he realized she might want the security offered by marriage, a legal promise of protection and care. "Yes, if that's what you wish."

She paused in her pacing and stared at him. "I'm not sure it is," she muttered. Her voice became sharper. "I hardly know how to cook. I can mend, but I'm hopeless at weaving. I would make you a terrible wife."

"You can learn those things."

"But I don't want to!" The words burst from her mouth, hot with frustration. "You don't understand. The life you're offering—it's exactly what I left. I grew up on a farm in the countryside, and I didn't much like it. Hispania, Italy—I don't think it makes much difference."

But this time, it would be with me. Was that not enough for her?

"Do you really have to go so far?" she demanded. "I don't see why you can't find land in Italy. Somewhere not so far from Rome."

He considered her words, attempting to view them rationally and disregard the ache spreading through his chest at the fact that she seemed to be rejecting him. It made sense she'd wish to stay in Italy. Her uncle was here. Maybe she didn't wish to be far from him. If she went to Hispania, she might never set foot here again.

Perhaps a compromise was in order. Though he'd set his sights on Hispania because it was the land of his birth, maybe, to keep Velia, he'd have to adjust his vision of the future.

"I would stay in Italy," he finally said. "If that's what it took for you to agree."

"You misunderstand me," she said quietly. "I meant…if you stayed in Italy, I could visit."

"Visit," he repeated, the word echoing around his skull. *Visit. She means to* visit *me? Not…* The ache in his chest intensified into a sharp, piercing pain that made the wound in his leg feel like he'd nicked himself while shaving.

Velia sat on the edge of his bed and reached for his hand, her small fingers closing around his. In the dark, her eyes glimmered with gathering tears.

"Ferox," she murmured. "I…" She swallowed hard. "I love you. But I don't love the life you're offering me."

He let out a long breath. She loved him. But somehow, it wasn't enough. "You would really rather stay here, surrounded by gladiators and violence and death, than come with me? I can offer you peace, Velia. Somewhere quiet, somewhere that just belongs to us."

"I don't want peace! I *like* it here, Ferox. I was only supposed to be here for a month, but I stayed because I found something here that I never knew existed. All my life I thought the only future for me was getting married, bearing children, spending my life caring for them and my husband. It felt like I was going to suffocate every time I thought of it. But Lucullus showed me there's another way. There's more I can want, different choices I can make."

"That's the difference," Ferox said sharply. "You *chose* this life. I didn't."

She was silent for a moment. The scraps of light caught on a tear sliding down her cheek. "You could choose it now," she whispered unsteadily.

"No," he said. "I can't stay here. This time when I leave, it will be forever." Though it would be difficult to leave Jason and Lea—and it might kill him to leave Velia—he needed a life free of ghosts, of guilt. A life that was truly his own.

He still prayed she would change her mind, that the prospect of such finality would sway her. But deep down, he knew her decision was made.

She wiped a hand across her eyes. "Very well," she murmured. "Excuse me. I should fetch you some fresh bandages." She rose from the bed and slipped from the room before he could say anything further.

25

V ELIA LEANED AGAINST THE wall outside Ferox's room. She squeezed her eyes shut, but tears still leaked from beneath her lids.

She should have known this conversation was coming. She'd been pretending that the end of Ferox's contracted time could arrive and they'd go their separate ways without a fuss. With regret, yes, but without this searing pain that felt as if it was going to tear her in two.

But after the events of last week—after Ferox *killed* for her—she should have known there would be a reckoning. It didn't matter if the emperor expelled him tomorrow, or if he fought his final match. Things had changed between them.

Somehow, though, this conversation snuck up on her with the unsettling shock of missing a stair.

He wanted her to come to Hispania with him. To be some sort of…*wife?*

She thought he knew her better than that. *Understood* her better than that.

In turn, she should have known better than to hope he'd stay in a life he hadn't chosen, a life that held only painful memories. There was no future for them. She'd been deluding herself to think this could end any other way.

Velia mopped the tears from her eyes with a fold of her dress, then gathered herself and headed outside. No matter her disappointment with him, his bandages still needed changing. She'd fetch some clean supplies from the storeroom and hope that by the time she reentered his room, she could face him without crying.

Dawn was just beginning to break, its light glowing over the eastern wall of the ludus. A figure approached from the other side of the courtyard, and Velia paused when she recognized her uncle, a habitual early riser. "Good morning, uncle."

He returned the greeting, but frowned when he caught sight of her face. "Is all well? Ferox—" His brows drew together in concern.

"He's fine," she interrupted. "Better, in fact. His fever has broken. I was just going to fetch a change of bandages."

The graveness didn't leave his face. "I would speak with you first."

"Very well." She followed Lucullus to his office, wondering what he could need at this early hour of the morning.

Lucullus closed the door behind them and turned to face her. A lamp had been left lit in the room, and its light flickered over her uncle's lined face, intensifying the crags and shadows. There was a dark, reluctant look in his eyes.

Unease spiraled through Velia. Her heart beat faster. *Something's wrong.* "What is it?"

"There was a messenger from the emperor," Lucullus said.

Velia drew in a sharp breath. "So early?"

Lucullus shook his head. "It came days ago. With Ferox ill, I thought perhaps it wouldn't matter."

If Ferox died, he meant. She swallowed hard. "So, is he to leave? Has the emperor expelled him from the games?"

"No."

"Oh." Relief hovered, tempting her to give in to it, but her uncle still looked much too solemn. "Then…what was the message?"

"The emperor would like Ferox to fulfill his final match, and has dictated the terms of that match. And the opponent."

Velia's breathing was choppy. Her mind raced as Lucullus spoke, conjuring all sorts of horrible possibilities. What did that mean? Was the emperor going to set up some sort of match where Ferox was destined to lose? Put him in the arena with no weapons, no armor? Was this the emperor's revenge for Ferox's defiance?

Lucullus continued. "The match will be against Achilles, and it will be to the death."

The room tilted. Black spots burst before her vision. Then, she was sitting, Lucullus having helped her into a chair. But she was still shaking, unable to draw breath, as her mind absorbed the awful implications of her uncle's words.

Ferox. Fighting Achilles. To the death.

One of them would die. Either the gladiator she'd invested so much in, or the one she loved.

She blinked dumbly at the floor, her vision still blotchy. Ordinarily, this match could only have one outcome—Ferox's victory. But with him so recently injured, weakened after an illness, and with Achilles having finally come into his own as a fighter…things were far less certain.

"Why?" she gasped.

Lucullus shrugged. "Everyone knows Ferox has been training Achilles. There is intrigue in pitting a student against a teacher. And everyone saw what Ferox did in his last match."

She understood her uncle's unspoken words. No matter what happened, this was a punishment for Ferox's defiance. Either he died, or he'd have to kill his own student.

Nausea roiled in her stomach. If Achilles died, she'd lose all the time and money she'd invested in him. He had only just begun to turn a profit. She'd have to start from scratch with a new fighter. Besides, even though she didn't particularly *like* Achilles, she felt a sense of responsibility for him. If he died, it would be her fault.

And—worst of all—she suspected Ferox would never forgive himself for killing Achilles. Two years later, Ferox still harbored guilt over his friend's death. His self-reproach if he swung the sword that killed Achilles would be a thousand times stronger.

But the alternative was too dreadful to contemplate.

Velia took a deep breath, trying to calm her body's trembling. "When?"

"Next week."

Another shudder ran through her. Precious little time for Ferox to recover. "That's not fair," she protested. "He won't even have his stitches out!"

Lucullus surveyed her. His gaze was cool, remote, as if they weren't discussing the fate of two men each crucial to her in their own ways. "I believe this is the only way it *is* a fair fight," he said. "You know Achilles can't hope to hold his own against Ferox at full strength. The injured master against the up-and-coming student…it does have a certain balance."

Velia curled her body forward, pressing her hands against her eyes as if by blinding herself she could block out all knowledge of this horrible situation. "You speak as if you don't care about them."

"Achilles is not my concern, and Ferox was never going to stay past this match, anyway." His words were cold, but he laid a hand on her shoulder, and she felt a hesitant tenderness behind the gesture. "Velia, if you're going to pursue this business, you must learn detachment. You're going to spend your life watching people you see and speak to every day be injured. Sometimes killed. You're going to see them suffer and struggle. You can't afford to let it break you. If you can't handle that, maybe this life isn't for you."

Lucullus's words cut through her shock and dread. "I understand." *You can handle this. You* must *handle this.* If she couldn't, then she'd have no choice but to return to her parents' farm, where eventually she'd wake up to discover she'd been married off to one of their neighbors.

This life might test her, but that life was intolerable.

She gathered her legs beneath her and forced herself to rise to her feet, though she still felt unsteady. "I'll inform Achilles. And if you'll permit me, I'll inform Ferox as well." She bore responsibility for this whole situation, so it was her duty to undertake the awful task of telling them both.

"Very well."

Achilles would likely be eating breakfast around now. Better to get this over with, so she nodded to her uncle, then left his office.

26

H ER STEPS HEAVY WITH dread, Velia made her way to the hall where the gladiators took their meals. It was nearly empty at this early hour, but Achilles was there, tucking into a bowl of steaming barley porridge.

She slid into the seat across from him. "I need to talk to you."

He raised his eyebrows as he shoveled another spoonful of porridge into his mouth. "Then talk," he said through a mouthful of food.

She hesitated, trying to find the words. "Your next match…the emperor has commanded…it will be against Ferox. And it will be to the—to the death." She swallowed hard after forcing out the terrible mandate.

He paused, the spoon halfway to his mouth. She eyed him warily, unsure how he'd react. In any other situation, this would be a death sentence for him.

His arm lowered, returning the spoon to the bowl. "When?"

"Next week."

Achilles leaned back, a considering look in his eyes. "All right."

Velia frowned. "All right? I've just told you that you'll have to face the man who trained you, the man who *made* you, in a fight to the death, and all you have to say is 'all right?'"

Achilles shrugged. "If you told me it was to be two weeks, or three, or a month…then I'd be packing my things and fleeing in the night. But now…" A touch of excitement flared in his eyes. "I have a chance. Imagine if I beat him, the great Ferox. My fame would explode. People would speak of it for years!"

Velia's stomach twisted. "You can't really be thinking of killing him."

He returned to his meal, his appetite seemingly reinvigorated. "It's either him or me, isn't it? That's what the emperor has decreed."

A thread of an idea occurred to her, and in desperation she clung to it. "Listen." She snatched the bowl away from him, ignoring his squawk of protest. "You must know you're still at a disadvantage. Even injured, Ferox is ten times the fighter you are."

He scowled at her. "Thanks."

"I know he won't want to kill you," she continued. "What if you both agree not to kill each other?"

Achilles grabbed for his bowl back, but she held it out of his reach. "The emperor ordered it to be a death match," he said. "I'm not stupid enough to defy that."

"But Ferox is leaving anyway after this match." Hope sprouted within her. Maybe, just maybe, if Achilles agreed…she could save them both. "He has nothing to lose by disobeying the emperor. So if you were to throw the fight, let him win…I know he'd swear not to kill you."

Achilles finally succeeded in clasping his fingers around the edge of the bowl. He yanked, and they wrestled for a moment before his superior strength wrenched it from her grasp. "You talk as if I'm afraid of dying."

"Aren't you?"

"If the gamble is between dying or winning more glory than I ever could have dreamed of less than two months into this…I'll take the bet."

"Please," she said desperately. "I can't lose either of you."

He gave her a dispassionate glance. "I'm not going to throw the fight, Velia. I know the odds may be still against me, but if I have the chance, I'll kill him. No mercy."

His words made her feel sick, but there seemed to be nothing left to say. Achilles's eyes were steely with determination, and he seemed entirely unfazed by the prospect of death.

"Fine," Velia sighed. She rose to her feet and turned toward the exit.

"Twelve mourners," Achilles called from behind her. "We agreed on it, remember?"

She gave him a short nod. He had indeed negotiated twelve mourners in the event of his death, but she'd hoped the promise wouldn't become relevant for a while yet. "Twelve mourners," she acknowledged in a low voice, then left the hall.

Velia went to the storeroom to complete her initial errand, fetching clean bandages for Ferox's wound. She'd begun it less than an hour ago, but already it felt like another life. A life before this terrible decree, this impossible choice.

She knew the emperor intended to punish Ferox with this final match, but it felt like a punishment targeted specifically at Velia. Gaius Caesar, of course, didn't even know she existed. He didn't care about what these two men meant to her, didn't care that losing either of them would destroy either her ambitions or her heart.

With the bandages in hand, she trudged back to Ferox's room, feeling as if she were the one who would face death in a week.

He was sitting up in bed when she entered, occupied in carefully peeling off the bandages to examine the puckered wound beneath. He glanced up at her, and his brows drew together. "Velia, about earlier—"

She held up a hand. "Please don't." She couldn't bear to revisit that conversation, couldn't add yet another thing that would tear at her heart.

He fell silent. She approached the bed and set about removing the rest of his bandages, tossing them aside. Her hands trembled as she replaced them with clean ones, wrapping the strips of fabric tightly as the physician had shown her. She'd done this many times over the past week, when Ferox had been sweating and senseless with fever. She knew the motion, her hands well-trained.

But now, her shaking fingers fumbled with the fabric, and her vision grew blurry. A tear dropped onto the cloth. She bent her head lower, trying to hide her tears, but Ferox's large hand found her face. His thumb slipped in the dampness on her cheek as he gently tilted her face up.

"I'm sorry about earlier," he murmured. "I never meant to upset you. I shouldn't have brought it up."

She closed her eyes, clasping his hand to her face. How many more times would she be able to feel his touch? "It's not that," she whispered, her voice raspy and unsteady.

"Then what is it?"

She returned her attention to his leg and finished securing the cloth in place with a tight knot, then perched on the edge of the bed. He moved over, making room for her, and she allowed herself to curl against his chest. Maybe this would be easier if she couldn't see his face. "I just spoke with my uncle. Apparently, there was a message from the emperor a few days ago. He waited until your fever had broken to share it."

Beneath her head, she felt the muscles of his chest and stomach stiffen. "The emperor is expelling me from the games." The words were resigned, flat—absent of surprise or anger.

She shook her head, her braid brushing his skin. "Worse." She closed her eyes and forced the words out. "He wants you to fight your last match. Next week. To the death. Against…Achilles."

He was silent for several long moments, the only sound the thump of his heartbeat in Velia's ear.

"I see," he finally murmured.

She straightened. His face was blank of emotion. Between Ferox, Achilles, and Lucullus, why was she the only one so rattled, so nearly broken by what was happening around her?

"Does Achilles know?" Ferox asked.

She nodded. "I just told him. I tried to get him to agree to let you win. I thought I could convince you not to kill him, no matter what the emperor orders. You have nothing to lose. You're leaving anyway. But he wouldn't agree!" Desperation sharpened her voice.

"You shouldn't have suggested that," Ferox chided. "Asking a gladiator to throw a fight—it's not honorable."

"I don't care about honor!" She launched herself off the bed. "I care about keeping you both *alive*. Can't you see what losing either of you would do to me? If Achilles dies, I lose everything I've put into him. He's barely profitable. I'd have to start over. His death would be on my conscience forever. And if you die—" She shook her head wordlessly.

Ferox swung his legs over the edge of the bed, planting his feet on the floor, but didn't rise. "If Achilles dies, you'll take everything you've learned and acquire a new gladiator. Yes, it will be a setback, but nothing you can't handle. If I die…" He spoke the words as coolly as if they were discussing the potential for rain that day. "You'll mourn me for a time, perhaps, but then you'll go on. You'll find a better man. One who can love you the way you want to be loved."

"I don't want a better man," she snapped. Words, hot and angry, rushed from her mouth in a torrent. "I want *you*. I want you to stay in Rome. I want you to train each and every one of my gladiators for the next ten, twenty, thirty years. I want you alive. I want you in my bed every night and by my side every day. I don't want you to die in the arena fighting fucking *Achilles!*"

He stared at her, his gaze dark and inscrutable. Then he glanced away, saying nothing.

Velia took an indignant step closer to the bed. "Why don't you *care* about any of this? Achilles was the same. Why am I the only one who feels like my heart is being ripped out of my chest?" She crossed her arms. "Tell me, how would you feel if the positions were reversed? Say, if I were about to face Penthesilea in the arena at the emperor's command?"

He gave her a sharp look. "That's completely different."

"Tell me," she pressed. "Tell me how you'd feel. Tell me what you'd do."

A muscle pulsed in his jaw. His brows lowered, casting a shadow over his face. "I'd take you away from here. We'd be out of the city before anyone even noticed we were gone. We'd go as far as possible. I'd take you to the wilds of bloody Britannia if that's what it took to keep you safe."

"So why not do the same for yourself?" she demanded. "You can leave. Run. You have nothing to lose."

"And would you come with me?"

The question hung in the air. Velia ground her teeth. "I'm not the one whose life is at stake."

"I'm not going to run, Velia," he said quietly. "There's no honor in fleeing a fair fight. And this fight with Achilles—it will be well-matched, given the circumstances." He brushed a hand over his bandaged leg. "Besides, if I fled, do you think the emperor would just give up? He'd blame Lucullus for my defection. He could take out his anger on your uncle, you, he could even disband the entire ludus if it pleased him. I won't have you all suffer for my cowardice."

Velia wanted to protest, but she couldn't argue with his reasoning.

"This fight will happen," Ferox continued. He heaved himself to his feet, coming toward her. Instinctually, Velia reached for him, wanting to steady him, and caught him by the arms.

His palms cupped her face. "It's out of your hands now, Velia," he murmured. "Please, if there's one thing you can do for me, don't distress yourself worrying. Don't try to convince me or Achilles to throw the fight or flee or whatever else comes into your head. It's in the hands of the gods now. There's nothing more you can do."

Anxiety and dread still tumbled in her stomach. *It's out of your hands*. His words were meant to give her relief, but she felt only helplessness at the thought of what was to come. But for his sake, she could pretend to fulfill his request. She gave a shaky nod. "I understand."

He kissed her on the forehead, and she released a long, heavy breath.

27

WHEN VELIA LEFT TO obtain some breakfast for them both, Ferox kept pacing his room. His thigh ached, and he longed to return to the comfort of his bed, but after the news Velia brought, he forced himself to remain upright. He needed to get his strength back as quickly as possible.

Ferox had summoned all the detachment he could muster in front of Velia. He wouldn't upset her more than she already was. It was best if she believed he could face this with complete equanimity. Treat it the same as any other fight.

He almost admired the emperor's ingenuity in devising this retribution. Likely, the man thought Ferox and Achilles were much closer to friends than they were in reality. But even though Ferox found Achilles extremely irritating most of the time, he still felt a sense of ownership over the novice. Achilles's wins and losses seemed to belong equally to Ferox, and if the novice were to die at Ferox's hand…

Ferox wasn't sure he'd be able to live with himself if he killed the man he'd spent countless hours shaping into a passable gladiator. And Velia might never forgive him, even if she knew he had no choice. Ferox meant what he said to her: he'd give this fight his all, come what may.

But that might be irrelevant if Achilles killed him first.

He had to turn his focus to regaining his strength. This would be his last fight ever, one way or another, and he wouldn't shame himself or his memory by limping into the arena like a weakling.

He spent the next day walking laps around the training area. His pace was slow and shuffling at first, but with the aid of a few hearty meals, the strength he'd lost from the week of illness returned. Then he had only to contend with the pain and weakness in his left leg. He ignored the pain as best he could, even when it rose to an all-consuming ache by the end of each day, and stretched the muscle between bouts of training, hoping to restore some pliability to the injured flesh.

The day before the match, he sparred with Lea late in the afternoon. Her blunted sword jabbed him in the ribs, and he stumbled back a step. That strike would have been fatal in the arena.

"You win," he conceded, breathing hard.

Lea tossed her sword to the ground. "Let's have a drink." She walked over to a bench on the perimeter of the training area and sat, reaching down for the jug of water and cups that rested on the ground nearby.

Ferox followed her, suppressing a hiss of relief as he took the weight off his injured leg. Lea poured them each a cup of water. He gulped his down with a murmur of thanks. Then, he retrieved the jug and poured the rest of its contents over his leg. Though the coolness only lasted a moment, it was still a blessed release from the burning pain. He would have killed for a trip to the frigidarium, the cold-plunge room at the baths, but he didn't want to be seen limping through the streets before his final match.

On the other side of the training area, Achilles battered a punching bag, his back to them. Ferox mentally corrected his form, but forced himself to glance away. They seemed to have a tacit agreement not to speak to each other since the news. It was best that way. They were no longer trainer and novice, but opponents.

Unfortunately, they knew each other's fighting styles better than any usual opponents would. Achilles's left-handed maneuvers wouldn't ruffle Ferox, but Achilles also knew Ferox's own quirks and tricks. They would be all too well-matched, and if not for the emperor's decree that the match be to the death, Ferox would have bet every sestertius he possessed on a draw.

His gaze shifted to Velia, standing near the entrance to the ludus. She was talking to the merchant who supplied the ludus with barley and flour. Tension gripped Ferox's body, but he shoved the feeling aside. He knew this merchant to be peaceable and inoffensive. Not like the stranger who had attacked Velia.

Nevertheless, Ferox kept his eyes on her.

Lea must have followed the direction of his gaze. "This is all for her, isn't it?" she murmured. "Yet I've barely seen you exchange two words in the past few days."

"This isn't her fault." But Lea was right about the fact that he and Velia had only spoken out of necessity. They certainly hadn't spent any nights together since he woke from his fever. He wanted desperately to go to her, to speak to her and soothe whatever worries he knew she had, but he hadn't been able to bring himself to approach, even though their time together was running out.

Maybe this was the least painful way for it to end—fizzling out in days of silence and avoidance.

"I didn't mean I blame her for it," Lea said. "Only that I wonder how you can defy the most powerful man in the world for someone and then, a week later, pretend she doesn't exist."

Ferox released a sigh. "I'm beginning to think dying may be the simplest outcome to all this." He imbued the comment with dark sarcasm.

"Did she ask you to throw the fight? Did you argue?"

Ferox shook his head. "Not about that. When I woke from my fever, I told her I wanted her to come with me to Hispania. I told her I would marry her. But she doesn't wish to leave this place."

Lea made a noise of scathing mirth. "Normal women want marriage and children and things like that. Velia is not a normal woman, Ferox. If that's what you want, you need to look else-where."

"That's not what I want," he snapped. "I don't care about marriage. I don't give a fig about children. I want *her*. I only offered because I thought—I thought it would help her say yes." But he'd been a fool. He'd known from his first sight of her that Velia was no ordinary woman. Ordinary women didn't choose to live in a ludus or work to acquire their very own gladiators.

So when he'd offered her an ordinary life, her refusal shouldn't have surprised him. "She asked if I might consider staying near-by. So she could *visit*." He tried to keep the bitterness from his voice.

Lea was silent for a moment. "What's left for you in Hispania? I doubt you'll even recognize the place. Your family is gone. What do you expect to find?"

That was a question he somehow hadn't considered. Lea's words forced him to admit to himself that he hadn't been thinking particularly far ahead. His entire plan comprised leaving the ludus and returning to Hispania because it was the only place other than Rome he knew.

Velia had finished talking with the merchant, who departed, so Ferox allowed his gaze to return to Lea. "I don't know," he muttered. "I just want to…not be here."

"Because of Hector?"

The sound of the name made him flinch. "You of all people should understand."

Lea raised an eyebrow. "What's that supposed to mean?"

Ferox hesitated, but he might be dead in a day's time. He could afford to finally confirm his suspicions about Lea and Hector. "You and Hector…you were lovers."

Her gaze slid away from his. She shifted on the bench, drawing one ankle up to rest on her opposite knee. "Yes, we were sleeping together. But we weren't…lovers." She grimaced at the word.

Ferox's incomprehension must have shown on his face, for she sighed. "We were friends who enjoyed bedding each other," she elaborated, which hardly helped. "We didn't *love* each other. Not in that way. Not like…" Her gaze shifted to Velia, now talking to Achilles.

Ferox still didn't understand—he had only ever had three friends in his life and had never been tempted to sleep with any of them—but he set it aside. "Even so. You knew him in a way Jason and I didn't."

Her voice softened. "The memories don't have to be something you need to escape from, you know. Yes, sometimes it's painful when I stop in front of what used to be his room and think, just for a moment, I can hear him humming to himself inside. Or when I see someone out of the corner of my eye who bears a passing resemblance to him but when I look, it's not him. But those little moments…they keep him alive, in a way. If memories are the only thing I have left of him, then I'll hold them close."

Ferox took a moment to absorb her words. It was tempting to view things as she did. To allow himself to bask in the memories instead of fleeing from them. But he couldn't. He didn't deserve to. "It's different for you," he said, his voice lowering. "It's not your fault he died."

"Neither is it yours."

"It is," Ferox grunted. "If I'd fought that day as I was supposed to, he would still be alive."

"Oh, stop it." Lea tossed her braid over her shoulder. "Velia thinks your match with Achilles is all her fault, doesn't she? There are some who might agree with her. But you would never allow her to believe that. Why can't you give yourself the same grace?"

Ferox blinked. He had never seen the two situations as remotely similar. In his mind, he alone was responsible for this match-up with Achilles, as he'd been the one to swing the sword that defied the emperor's wishes.

But if that were true…could he view Hector's death the same way? Could he admit the only person truly responsible was the man who'd actually killed him?

"I don't think Hector sees it that way," Ferox muttered.

Lea gave him a questioning glance.

Ferox hesitated; he hadn't wanted to bring this up, but perhaps it was too late for such circumspection. "I've felt him haunting me," he confessed. "I have these dreams of him in the underworld, all bloodied and wounded. I know he's angry with me. He blames me for his death."

The confession, painful as it was, eased something in his chest. This had been his burden to bear for so long, and there was relief in sharing it, even if it wouldn't fix anything.

"You blame *yourself* for his death," Lea said. "That's where those dreams come from. Listen to me." She swiveled on the bench to face him. "Hector didn't relish this life. For better or for worse, he's at peace now. No more fighting, no more violence. He's *happy* now."

The conviction in her voice tempted him. What if she was right? What if his dreams were merely the result of his own misplaced guilt, not Hector's shade seeking to torment him?

"Hector is not haunting you," Lea continued. "You're haunting yourself. Hector is off frolicking in Elysium. I doubt he even spares us a thought. And if he does, you know he'd want us all to be happy. Even if you had wronged him, he wasn't the sort to hold a grudge."

That was true. Hector would forgive nearly anything. Once, Ferox had witnessed Hector get into a fistfight with a man who'd insulted his accent. Hector had bludgeoned the man into submission, then a quarter of an hour later, they'd been deep into a game of dice, laughing and chatting as if they were the best of friends. Hector didn't hesitate to solve problems with his fists, but he also was quick to forgive.

Ferox abruptly realized the version of Hector conjured by his guilt bore little resemblance to the real man.

You're haunting yourself.

"Listen, you have many strengths, but you're not exactly the most agile thinker," Lea said. "You get one idea in your thick head and you cling to it as if it's the only thing that's true. Hector dies, you decide to leave the ludus with barely the clothes on your back. A terrible idea, as Jason and I tried to tell you. How did that go?"

"Not well," Ferox admitted.

"Then you come back, and all you can think about is this even more terrible idea of abandoning everyone who cares about you for a place you haven't been in what, fifteen years? And you talk about wanting to buy a farm or a vineyard or a mine or whatever it is—but you know nothing about any of that, do you?"

Ferox stared at the ground. Maybe he had made some poor decisions in the past, motivated by a guilt which—if he could believe Lea—might have been misplaced. Maybe he was on the verge of another terrible decision.

"If Hector hadn't died, would you have still wanted to leave?" she asked.

"No," he muttered. Ferox had never considered leaving until Hector's death. He'd been…if not precisely happy, then content. He had a better life than many in this very city. Once he got too old to fight, assuming he hadn't met his death in the arena, he probably would have convinced Lucullus to repurpose him as a trainer for the newer gladiators. Just like he was doing now, for Velia.

"I don't begrudge you wanting something different," Lea said. "None of us ended up here by choice, after all. But that doesn't mean it's impossible to build something real." She fell silent, and her gaze grew faraway. "My mother's favorite plant was the thistle."

Ferox blinked at the incongruous remark, but stayed quiet, trusting she had a reason to mention it.

"She liked their purple flowers, but it was mostly because of how their seeds work," Lea continued. "The wind carries the seeds far and wide, and they grow wherever they land. She used to say if a little thistle could make the best of wherever it found itself, then so could we."

Ferox made a low murmur of acknowledgment. Lea rarely spoke of her past, but he knew she'd been enslaved with her mother, who died shortly before Lea ended up at the ludus.

"Do you understand what I mean?" she asked.

Ferox nodded. She meant he could be like a thistle. He could put down roots where he found himself, choose to make this life his own.

But in order to do that, he'd first have to believe Lea, believe her conviction that Hector was at peace, not haunting him. That he bore no responsibility for Hector's death, just as Velia bore no responsibility for the circumstances of this upcoming fight. That what seemed like Hector's ghost was just Ferox's own misplaced guilt.

As he attempted to get his head around the idea, Nyx prowled up to them. The cat's yellow gaze swung from Lea to Ferox, and he emitted a hiss in Ferox's direction. Then he darted forward and swatted at Ferox's foot.

Ferox jerked his foot back with haste.

"He wants you to leave," Lea said helpfully.

Ferox grumbled, but he'd rested for long enough. He needed to get back to training. He heaved himself from the bench, and as soon as the spot was vacant, Nyx hopped up and rubbed his face against Lea's arm.

Ferox picked up his sword and went to find another sparring partner, contemplating thistles and seeds and roots as he did.

28

VELIA EYED HER BED doubtfully. Night had fallen, but she hadn't yet extinguished her lamp. She knew she wouldn't be able to sleep tonight, the night before Ferox and Achilles fought to the death, and there seemed to be little point in trying.

Dread had been pooling in her stomach all day, steadily intensifying until it felt like it gripped her with a dozen pairs of grasping, crushing hands.

No matter what happened tomorrow, it would be the worst day of her life.

Her gaze shifted to the door, her thoughts turning to Ferox. She'd been trying to summon the courage to go to him since dusk. Surely, they couldn't spend this night apart.

But she must be more of a coward than she realized, for the prospect of seeing him terrified her. It was the reason she'd stayed away from him these past few days. She feared the pain and grief it would bring, feared being broken under their weight. What was she even to say to him?

Perhaps he didn't want to see her. He'd been avoiding her too, after all. Perhaps seeing her would cloud his judgment tomorrow, would weaken him.

She sat on her bed but jumped up a moment later as nervous energy propelled her to pace her tiny room.

Just open the door and walk to his room, she urged herself. *You'll regret it forever if you let him leave or die without spending this last night with him.*

She took one step toward the door—and then the sound of a knock stopped her in her tracks.

She forced herself into motion, found the handle of the door, and pulled it open.

Ferox stood in the corridor. She couldn't see his face in the shadows, but before she could stammer a greeting, he was inside her room. The door swung shut behind him. His arms encircled her, pulling her into a desperate, greedy embrace. She didn't have to see his face to feel the need in his touch.

She clutched at him. Maybe she shouldn't have worried about what to say to him. Maybe tonight, the time for words was past.

He pressed her backward until his body pinned her against the wall. Her head spun with desire, mounting quickly in a hot rush over her skin. Their lips met in a hard, urgent kiss.

He pulled away after only a moment. "Velia," he growled, his hands gripping her waist. "I warn you, I don't have gentleness in me tonight. So if you want me to leave, tell me now."

Tonight, she wanted everything he could give her. She wanted his roughness, his hunger, his lust. She hooked one leg around his to draw their bodies even closer. His arousal, already stiff, jutted against her, kindling even more desire.

"Don't leave," she whispered.

With a groan, he lowered his head to capture her mouth once more. His kiss was fierce, desperate—no softness to it. Velia gave his fierceness back to him by sinking her teeth into his bottom lip. His body jerked, and he broke off from the kiss with a gasp.

His hand settled at the base of her throat, fingers wrapping around it. The possessive grasp, heavy but not crushing, made need pulse between her legs.

"One more thing," he whispered, voice raspy and uneven. "I'd be a fool to think I have the control to withdraw. Not tonight. So again, if you don't want that—"

"I have my herbs." Besides, she knew her courses approached in the coming days, and understood that was the time in her monthly cycle when she was least likely to conceive. This time—the last time—with Ferox, she was willing to take that risk.

He kissed her once more. His hands divested her of her dress, then roved over her bare body. She leaned into his touch, arching against him as his fingers delved between her legs.

A low, approving noise rumbled in his chest when his fingers slipped in her wetness. Then he grabbed her around the waist, and suddenly she was on the other side of the room, perched atop her narrow chest of drawers.

He dropped to his knees before her. His hands slid beneath her bottom, yanking her to the edge of the surface.

"Oh!" Velia tilted her hips forward, leaning her shoulders against the wall to give him better access as he buried his face between her legs.

There was no gentle build of sensation, no slow, careful pleasuring. His mouth was relentless on her. After so many times together, he knew exactly what to do to make her shudder and quake. He worked her with unsparing focus. She was powerless, unable to do anything but clench her thighs around his head as he conquered her with his mouth.

The climax crashed over her in an all-consuming, merciless wave. For those blissful moments, she forgot where she was, forgot the dread of tomorrow, even forgot her own name.

When it subsided, she slumped against the wall, dazed by the pleasure still swirling through her body, enveloping her in a blissful fog.

Ferox gave her no time to recover. He rose to his feet, shucked off his tunic, and grabbed her hips. Then, before she could even take a breath, he buried himself inside her in one urgent thrust. She gasped, hands clutching at his shoulders. There was slight discomfort at his swift invasion, mixed with sharp sparks of residual pleasure. Her muscles quickly relaxed, well-accustomed to him after so many times together.

He paused for only the barest moment to slide his palms beneath her bottom, drawing her closer. Then he drove into her, once, again, again. She gripped his shoulders and held on, legs wrapping around his waist. His breath was harsh in her ear.

Ferox broke off to tweak her position again, his grasp rough and unyielding on her hips. Then, he withdrew suddenly with a sigh of frustration, as if he couldn't quite find the angle he wanted. He took hold of her waist and deposited her on the bed.

"This is what you like, right?" he growled as he bent one leg over her head.

"Yes—oh!" Her assent was swallowed up by a moan as he slid into her once more. Something about this position heightened every sensation. Her other leg curled around his hip, urging him even deeper. He set a demanding rhythm that soon had a fresh wave of pleasure building in her core. She tilted her hips, searching for more. "Don't stop," she begged. "Just—just like that."

A groan vibrated in his chest. "Again?" he panted. There was a note of incredulity in his voice, as if he couldn't believe she was actually enjoying this.

She nodded, her forehead bumping his shoulder. Her eyes fell shut, and she allowed the swelling pleasure to consume her entire focus. It burst with an intensity that was nearly painful, her muscles already well-used by his previous attentions. Her teeth sank into the flesh of his shoulder.

He let out a ragged grunt. His body shuddered, then collapsed on top of hers. She only felt his weight for a moment before he rolled off.

His arms found her, pulling her against his chest. She kept her eyes closed, reveling in only the sensations she could hear and feel: the slowing rhythm of his breath, the thump of his heart beneath her ear, the brush of his fingers on her arms.

Once she opened her eyes, the reality she'd been trying to escape from would intrude.

"I'm sorry," he murmured.

"For what?"

"I was a brute. I must have hurt you."

That got her to open her eyes. She half-turned to send him a skeptical look. "Did you miss the part where I climaxed twice?" Her body was still heavy with the remains of the pleasure he'd brought her.

He glanced away, abashed. "Still. I should have been gentler."

She rolled her eyes and returned to lie in his arms, her back pressed against his chest. As she feared, thoughts of tomorrow trespassed on her satisfied mind, chasing away the moment of ease. Icy dread gathered in her stomach once more.

Velia sat up, unable to enjoy Ferox's warmth. She caught sight of the curved red marks on his shoulder, wrought by her teeth. In a strange way, it pleased her he'd go into the arena tomorrow marked by her.

She swallowed hard. There was something she needed to say to him. Something that would take all her courage. "Ferox…about tomorrow…" She passed a hand through the remains of her braid, disentangling the segments that had survived the rough coupling until her fingers could slide through with no resistance.

His gaze fixed on her, and he waited in silence for her to speak.

"I don't want you to hold back," she finally said. "You have my blessing, if you need it, to win." *To kill Achilles.* In their last conversation, Ferox had said he wouldn't throw the fight, but she feared he wouldn't give it his all, out of care for her. So she wouldn't lose Achilles.

And Velia couldn't stand fearing *she* was the unwitting cause of Ferox's death.

"As terrible as it sounds," she said, "I can live with Achilles dying. I can start over if I have to." The words pained her, though they were true. She felt responsible for Achilles, aside from the potential money his career would bring her, and she didn't want his death on her conscience. She sensed she'd carry that guilt forever. But if the choice was between Achilles and Ferox…there was only one decision she could make.

"But you…" Velia continued. "I can't live with you dying."

His hand found hers, fingers twining together. "Even if you know I'll leave and you'll never see me again? It will be the same for you whether I live or die."

She shook her head. "Not the same. If you leave, I can imagine you being alive. Being happy. Not that I understand how you'd be happy, living in the middle of nowhere all by yourself." She intended the remark as a joke, but bitterness laced it.

He propped himself on an elbow, facing her. She didn't miss his wince as his injured leg shifted against the mattress. Unease joined the dread in her stomach. Her declaration didn't matter if Ferox actually found himself unable to best Achilles.

"I wouldn't be happy," he said. "Not without you."

"I haven't—haven't changed my mind," she said unsteadily. "I can't leave—"

"I'm not asking you to leave. I'm telling you I want to stay."

Velia held her breath, hardly able to comprehend his words. "You...what?"

"It's Lea's doing," he said gruffly. "She made me realize I'd been very stupid about several things. Thinking Hector's death was my fault. Believing he'd go to the trouble of haunting me. Planning to leave behind the closest thing I've had to a home since I was a child. And there was something about thistles..." He shook his head. "This will still be my last fight. But leaving you...well, the thought of it feels like severing my own arm."

Tears blurred her vision. She opened her mouth, but couldn't speak.

"Besides," he continued, "I hear there's a new manager who might need a trainer for her gladiators."

Emotion swelled in her chest. "I've heard the same thing," she managed with a wavering chuckle. She wanted to throw herself into his arms and weep with joy, but his words didn't erase what was about to happen tomorrow. He still had to fight, still had to face death. Now, if he lost, it would feel all the more cruel for being so close to happiness.

"I love you, Velia," he murmured, his voice roughening. "Whatever time I have left, I want to spend it with you."

29

FEROX DIDN'T BOTHER TRYING to sleep that night. He knew he wouldn't be able to, and he didn't want to waste a moment with Velia on sleep.

She eventually fell into a doze, and he lay as still as possible so he didn't wake her. He savored every rise and fall of her chest, every twitch of her body as she shifted. How had she grown so precious to him?

It seemed like yesterday that she was nothing more than a strange woman wheedling him into training her novice and telling him scandalous things about her past. Then again, the fact that he'd led an entire life without knowing her felt unthinkable. She'd burrowed herself so deeply into his heart, into his soul, that he couldn't take a breath without feeling her.

The light in the room turned grayish as the hours passed, and then the first golden rays of dawn slid through the small window. Velia stirred, stretching with a sigh. She rolled over to face him, her eyes still closed. Her knee lifted to settle atop his hip. "I want you again," she breathed.

Her proximity all night had made arousal simmer gently beneath his skin, and it flared to life at her words. He brought her beneath him, settling his body over hers. They were both still naked, and the brush of her bare skin made his cock swell to attention.

He slid a hand down to palm her sex. Her soft warmth made his mouth go dry with need. "Are you sure?" He worried she'd be sore from last night. But now, the frantic hunger that had possessed him then was sated. He could be slower, gentler this time.

She nodded. He stroked her until her arousal dewed his fingers. Then, he slid one finger inside her, his thumb rubbing at the apex of her quim. He knew he'd found the right spot when her breath caught. She squirmed beneath him, shifting restlessly. A flush crept from her cheeks down to her collarbone, echoing the pink of her nipples. Bathed in the dawn sunshine, it was the most beautiful sight he could imagine.

He increased the pressure of his fingers, just as he knew she liked. He'd learned her body well by now—he knew how to draw out the pleasure, spinning it longer and longer like thread on a spindle, or, alternately, how to make the climax crash over her as quick and intense as a thunderclap.

This morning, the latter approach was in order, and he devoted himself to driving her higher and higher, giving her every bit of pleasure he could.

A moan slipped from her lips, and she thrust a hand down to hold his in place. Tremors wracked her as she came apart beneath his hand, around his finger deep inside her.

His cock gave a demanding throb at the sight and feel of her climax. She'd liked it last night when he entered her right after she came, so he did the same now, notching himself at her entrance and easing himself inside. Her warmth gripped him, and he muffled a curse against her shoulder.

She brought her legs up to wrap around his waist, affording him even deeper access, and she let out a gasp as he buried himself to the hilt.

"Did I hurt you?" he grunted, struggling to get the words out amid the pleasure flooding him.

She slid her hands over his shoulders. "It's good," she reassured him.

Still, he proceeded cautiously, withdrawing and then sinking back into her with torturous slowness. He wanted to make this last as long as possible—but the slick, tight feel of her quickly unraveled his control.

Ferox gritted his teeth and held back the pleasure threatening to overwhelm him. He took her with as much restraint as he could muster, until he was shaking with need.

Only then did he allow himself to succumb to the pleasure grasping at every fiber of his mind and body. He shuddered, his movements growing rough as he rode out the explosive release. Velia's hands stroked over and over his shoulders, urging him on, until it finally subsided.

Ferox collapsed on his side next to her. He pulled her into his arms and pressed a kiss to her forehead. But even the comfort of her body couldn't block out the ache in his leg, reminding him what awaited him in a few short hours. He prayed he'd regained enough strength to do what needed to be done.

There was relief in knowing this would be his last fight. One last match that would decide everything. Either he perished, or he'd start a new life with Velia by his side.

The crowd roared as Ferox made his way into the arena. He walked slowly, testing the feel of his leg on the sand, which was looser and more unstable than the dirt of the practice area. His leg ached as it had since his injury, but so far, it felt strong.

His gaze, partially obscured by his helmet, swept toward the viewing area where the emperor and his entourage sat, near the row of white-swathed Vestal Virgins. The emperor was on his feet, leaning against the balustrade with a blue-glass goblet in his hand. He chatted with a woman beside him, both richly garbed in garments of purple trimmed with gold.

Ferox bet the emperor's mandate that the fight be to the death was not common knowledge. The audience would be excited enough for this match without that, and Ferox had a feeling the ruler would want to indulge in the drama of the life-or-death decision at the end of the match.

Ferox's mind went back to his first match of these games, less than two months ago. He'd been nervous then, fearing his long absence had sapped his skill. But his greatest fear had been that he'd embarrass himself. He'd known the chances of dying were slim.

Velia had been more anxious than he was. She'd made him promise not to die. He'd given the promise easily, knowing he'd be able to keep it.

Today, he could make no such promise, and Velia hadn't asked. She'd sent him off at the edge of the arena with one last fierce embrace, but that was it. No promises. No words at all, even. They'd already said everything that needed to be said.

The noise of the crowd swelled as Achilles made his way onto the sand from the arena's other side. He was helmetless, as he now always fought, his red hair his signature.

The volume of cheers for Achilles gratified Ferox. The novice had garnered himself a solid fanbase in his fledgling career.

As they both approached the center of the arena, where the official stood, Ferox pulled off his helmet and tossed it aside. A murmur of interest ran through the crowd.

He knew Achilles would fight without a helmet, and Ferox could have simply left his at the ludus, but he also knew the crowd would appreciate the drama of discarding it.

The official directed them into starting positions. Ferox adjusted his stance slightly, angling his body to better meet Achilles's left-handed attacks.

Their gazes joined across the short distance between them. Achilles's hazel eyes showed nothing but grim determination. Ferox knew, as he'd never questioned, that if he faltered, if his leg gave out on him, Achilles would show him no mercy.

The crowd quieted in anticipation. Ferox sank his feet deeper into the sand, seeking as much stability as possible. He guessed Achilles was going to strike quickly; there would be no cautious circling, no careful evaluation. They didn't need to take each other's measure, having sparred against each other dozens of times by now. Besides, Achilles sought the glory of defeating a celebrated gladiator; he'd want to show himself in control from the start.

At a shout from the official, the fight began. As Ferox anticipated, Achilles leaped forward immediately with a powerful thrust of his sword. A strike like that from a left-handed opponent might have thrown another fighter off-kilter, but Ferox caught the blow easily on his shield.

Achilles hopped back a half step, then struck again. Ferox batted his sword aside with his own weapon and pushed forward, managing a shallow slice to Achilles's upper arm. Achilles fell back, and Ferox gathered his strength for another quick thrust, but his leg wouldn't move as fast as he needed it to. By the time he crossed the two steps to meet Achilles again, the novice had his shield up and easily blocked the next strike.

They battled on, painfully well-matched. Achilles's lack of experience showed in occasional fumbling or graceless footwork, but Ferox failed to take advantage of those little missteps, unable to move quickly enough. Achilles scored a superficial cut to Ferox's abdomen. It bled freely, earning roars of delight from the crowd, but Ferox knew it looked worse than it was and wouldn't weaken him.

Soon, they were both breathing hard. Sweat gleamed on Achilles's skin, plastering his red hair to his forehead. Ferox's grip on his sword became slippery with sweat. Drawing each breath felt like hauling a heavy bucket of water from a well. They took longer and longer between strikes. Out of the corner of his eye, Ferox glimpsed the official step forward, as if to call a halt, but then hurriedly moved back. Ferox bet the emperor had signaled him to stand down. There would be no breaks, no draws.

With each lunge, each blow caught on his shield, Ferox's leg became weaker, until it trembled with every movement. This was dangerous: this was the point where Achilles's superior strength could outweigh his lack of experience and overcome Ferox.

Achilles knew it too, for Ferox could see the other man's eyes flicking toward Ferox's leg, as if assessing his remaining strength. Achilles let out a snarl and darted forward with renewed vigor.

The impact of Achilles's sword on Ferox's shield was too much for his leg to bear, and it collapsed beneath him.

If Ferox wanted any chance of surviving, he had to take Achilles down with him. Quick as he could, he tossed away his shield and clenched his now-free hand around Achilles's leather-covered forearm.

They tumbled to the sand together, swords clashing. Achilles's blade jabbed toward Ferox's throat. Ferox narrowly got his right arm up to block it. The blade came down on his forearm, glancing off the plate armor that covered it.

He discarded his own sword and used both hands to divest Achilles of his weapon. His left hand gripped the blade, which cut deep into his palm, and the other grasped Achilles's wrist in a crushing grip. The sword slipped from Achilles's fingers, and Ferox flung the weapon wide. Blood coated Ferox's left hand, and he gritted his teeth against the pain.

Sand flew as they wrestled. Ferox knew he had the advantage here; though they were matched in height, Ferox was much heavier than the novice. Also, on the ground like this, Ferox's weakened leg was less of a disadvantage.

Ferox could taste victory. Achilles was slowing, though he hadn't yet let himself be pinned.

Then, Achilles's knee slammed into the wound on Ferox's thigh. Agony erupted, and everything went white.

Dimly, through the searing pain, Ferox glimpsed Achilles's arm reaching for his nearby sword. If Achilles got his hands on that weapon, it was over.

Ferox used his uninjured leg to propel himself forward in a half-crawl, half-lunge. He scraped his hand through the sand, sending a spray into Achilles's eyes. The novice swore, his voice ragged and guttural. He fumbled for the sword, but blinded by the sand, couldn't find it.

Ferox grabbed the sword instead, his fingers closing around the grip. A moment later, Achilles was on his back, the point of the sword at his throat.

Ferox paused, breathing hard, on his knees crouching over Achilles. The roar of the crowd reverberated around his skull.

Slowly, the noise coalesced into something intelligible. *Mercy*, they shouted.

Ferox's eyes flicked toward the emperor, standing at the front of his box. The man surveyed the crowd. He held out a fist, thumb turned out.

The gesture for death.

The cries for mercy blurred into shouts of surprise. Ferox hesitated. His arm shook where it extended the sword. He just had to do this one thing. One strike, and it would all be over.

Achilles glared up at him, his face covered with sweat, sand, and blood. His gaze betrayed no fear. After the fight they'd just had, Ferox wasn't surprised that the prospect of death seemed like a relief.

"Just fucking do it," Achilles growled.

Ferox tightened his grip on the sword, muscles tensing as he prepared to drive it down. He could make it quick. Painless.

Achilles would be on the banks of the Styx before he could even blink.

But the noise of the crowd caught his attention once more. The clamor of surprise had turned into something else. Loud, insistent *boos* emanated from the stands, along with hisses and other more colorful jeers.

Ferox blinked. Never before had he heard the people express their displeasure with a decision.

His gaze returned to the emperor. Ferox couldn't see his face, but the man's fists were clenched where they rested on the balustrade. He turned his head, seeming to speak to the woman next to him.

"Do it," Achilles snarled again.

"Shut up," Ferox snapped. His eyes remained on the emperor as the man absorbed the noise of twenty thousand people booing him.

The emperor opened his arms, a magnanimous gesture. The intensity of noise from the crowd dissipated, replaced by a sense of anticipation, of held breaths as everyone waited to see what he would do next. Would he uphold his decision? Would he change his mind?

The emperor extended his arm. This time, the fist was closed, the thumb tucked inside. Mercy.

The crowd exploded with noise once more, though this time, it was cheers, celebration.

A jolt of relief nearly toppled Ferox. The sword fell from his grasp, and he only narrowly moved his arm so it didn't strike Achilles in the chest.

That would have been the height of irony—for Achilles to be spared by the emperor, only to be accidentally skewered by Ferox dropping his sword.

Ferox sat back on his heels. The sand beneath him seemed to tremble with the force of the noise that erupted from the crowd. Then Ferox realized he was the one shaking. With exhaustion, with weakness, with pain, with shock.

Achilles hauled himself into a sitting position, wiping sand from his face. His coppery brow was furrowed. He glanced from Ferox to the emperor, incomprehension clear on his face. He might have said something, but Ferox couldn't hear him amid the noise and the shambles of his own mind.

It was time to leave the arena, but standing was not an option at present. His legs felt like they were made of soft, unfired clay; they'd collapse under the slightest weight. The half-healed wound on his left leg bled freely, torn open by that vicious kick from Achilles.

Ferox eyed his sword. If he could drive it into the sand, maybe he could use it as leverage to rise—

Before he could reach for it, a pair of hands anchored under his arms. Achilles hauled him to his feet. "Get up, old man. Unless you want a front-row seat to the next match?"

Ferox managed a grunt in reply as they stumbled together to the arena's exit. As soon as the shadows of the passage fell over him, his wounded leg gave out once and for all. His weight slumped, too heavy for Achilles to catch. He braced himself to hit the ground, but there were other hands, other arms there to catch him. Lea and Jason, he realized dimly, as they supported him into the open area beyond the passage.

They eased him to the ground, his back against the wall. Sitting was a relief, though his leg still screamed in agony. There were other wounds, too—slices and aches and rips in his skin he didn't even remember getting.

He had no time to catalogue his injuries, for no sooner had his body reached the ground than Velia hurled herself into his arms. She wrapped her arms around him, clinging tight enough to crack a marble column. Her elbow was digging into a wound on his shoulder, but he didn't care. The pain was nothing compared to the pleasure of having her in his arms.

"You did it," she gasped amid sobs. "I-I can't believe it!"

He wanted to object that Achilles deserved the credit for his salvation; if the novice hadn't built such a reputation for himself, the crowd wouldn't have protested so strenuously at the emperor's decision. But Ferox wasn't yet capable of speaking, so he allowed himself to sink into her embrace. His left palm was a bloody mess, and he was probably ruining her clothing, but he couldn't bring himself to release her.

This was where he belonged. Anywhere Velia was. Whether she wanted to stay at the ludus forever or move to the underworld itself, he would follow her.

30

V ELIA SMILED AS HER feet sank into the three rugs that adorned the floor of Ferox's bedroom. The vestiges of the tension that had gripped her all day finally lifted at the sight of him, sitting up in bed and sipping a cup of water. Bandages covered him in several spots, but he was overall in one piece.

She still couldn't believe the day had turned out like this, that neither Ferox nor Achilles had died. She'd been frozen with fear for the entire match, which seemed to stretch for hours. When Achilles had landed that brutal kick to Ferox's wounded leg, she'd nearly collapsed in horror, her vision patchy and every muscle quivering like the last autumn leaf on a branch. She was sure that was it, that Achilles's sword would be at Ferox's throat in the next moment.

But somehow, Ferox had gotten the upper hand. Then, she'd watched in petrified awe as the emperor reversed his decision, conceding to the crowd's will.

She would never forget the sight of both of them stumbling from the arena, exhausted, bloodied, but alive.

The physician had tended to Ferox's leg with much displeased muttering. He had to remove the remnants of the previous stitches and close the wound once more. He'd warned that Ferox might be left with a limp.

Besides his leg, the slice on his left palm was the worst injury, and the physician had stitched that too before wrapping it tightly in bandages. His hand, like his leg, might never regain full mobility. Ferox had accepted both prognoses with a grim nod.

Now, Velia bore a tray of food covered with a napkin, which she set carefully on Ferox's lap.

He murmured thanks. "I heard a ruckus outside. Is anything amiss?"

Velia grinned wryly at the memory of the disturbance she'd just left. "Achilles is telling anyone who will listen that he let you win. Lea punched him in the mouth. Jason had to drag her off him."

"Gods below," Ferox muttered.

"No one believes him," Velia said. "Anyone who watched the match could see he was fighting for his life. But I could have watched Lea knock him on his backside ten times. Even though she shouldn't be punching anyone after—" Velia broke off. She didn't want to worry Ferox with details of what happened in Lea's match.

"After what?" he pressed, raising himself into a taller sitting position.

Velia hesitated, but he'd find out soon enough. "Lea was wounded earlier. She's fine," Velia added quickly when she saw the tension ripple through his large body, the worry flaring in his gaze. "She even won. The emperor was so impressed he called her up to his box and personally awarded her a prize. I think he was trying to give people something else to talk about after earlier."

"Did the physician tend to her?"

"You won't believe it, but the emperor sent his personal physician to see to her wound. He must have done a good job, since she was well enough to pummel Achilles." Velia had briefly caught sight of the man, and she grinned. His appearance had made quite the impression on her. "I think he's Greek, and he's *very* handsome."

Ferox glowered. "I don't need to hear about the other men you find handsome."

"I didn't say *I* found him handsome," Velia clarified. "Just that he was, objectively, handsome. Not that Lea seemed to notice." Velia ran a hand up Ferox's uninjured leg over the blanket, stopping when she reached the wooden tray still resting on his thighs. "Luckily for you, I prefer rugged, battle-scarred gladiators to devastatingly handsome Greek physicians."

"Now he's devastatingly handsome?" Ferox growled.

Velia let out a ringing laugh. "All right, he was the ugliest man I've ever seen. Happy?"

Ferox grumbled and turned his attention to the tray, removing the napkin that covered it. "What's this?"

Velia reached out to pick up one of the globi, the fried cheese-cake balls she'd acquired specially. "Lea told me about your conversation. How you've gone all this time thinking your friend was haunting you. I remembered you told me his favorite food was globi. So I thought, if he is here, maybe he'd like to know we remember him this way."

She hadn't realized the extent to which Ferox had been tormented by his grief and his guilt until speaking to Lea earlier that day. Her heart broke to think of how he must have suffered, stubbornly refusing to unburden himself to his friends because he believed he didn't deserve solace. Now, she hoped he would one day be able to remember Hector with fondness, not anguish.

A small smile lifted the corners of Ferox's mouth. He lifted one of the round golden morsels. "You know, I think I do feel him here, but not in the way I used to." He closed his eyes briefly. "I hope you're stuffing your face with these in Elysium, my friend," he murmured, then popped the ball into his mouth.

Velia joined him in devouring the rest of the globi, along with the other, more nutritious food she'd brought. As she ate, she surveyed him. Now that the all-consuming stress of the day was behind them, her mind turned toward the future.

They hadn't fully discussed Ferox's declaration that he'd stay and be her trainer, as things had still been so uncertain last night. What if he'd changed his mind? What if he'd only said it to make her happy in that moment, knowing he might not survive the next day?

"Did you…mean what you said last night?" she asked, cursing the hesitation in her voice. "Only because, well, if you're to stay, I'm going to have to pay my uncle for your room and board. So you'd better enjoy every bite of that food if it's coming out of my purse."

He polished off a chunk of cheese, then met her gaze. "I meant it."

Relief and joy flooded her in equal measure. An exuberant smile spread across her face. She'd thought this day was going to be the worst of her life, but it might just have become the best.

"I have one condition, though," he continued.

"Oh?" She couldn't think of anything he'd ask that she'd refuse.

"If you're to take on more gladiators, and I'm to train them…I want them all to be volunteers. Like Achilles. No slaves." His eyes were dark and serious.

Velia nodded without hesitation. "Only volunteers." Limiting herself to volunteers would slow her ability to expand, as she'd have to wait for the right candidates to present themselves, but she understood why Ferox asked that, and it was easy to agree.

"I'll have to put the word out that I'm looking for men," she said. "I was hoping to make enough profit to move into a ludus of our own in the next year or so. There's an empty building nearby that I think is the right size. It would take some patching up, but it would do."

He twined his fingers with hers. "Whatever figure you think you'll need to raise, subtract thirty thousand from it. I still have the earnings from my first fight. Well, minus the rugs you made me buy. And that pitcher."

"You'd really do that? Spend your money on buying a new ludus?"

"Not just a ludus," he murmured. "A future. With you."

Tears welled, and she dashed them away with the back of her hand. "Well, if you're to be my trainer, that makes you my employee," she announced, laughing through her lingering tears. "Which means you have to do *everything* I say." She allowed her smile to turn sly, suggestive.

His eyebrows twitched. "We'll see about that."

She glanced at the bandages visible on his hand and elsewhere. "I don't think you're in any condition to be giving orders."

Heat sparked in his gaze. "Take this tray away and I'll show you what condition I'm in."

She reached for the tray but bit her lip. A familiar throbbing tingle was building in her core, but despite her saucy words, she knew they may need to hold back until he had recovered further. "Are you sure? We can wait…"

"Put the tray on the floor, Velia."

When he took that dark, commanding tone, there was no denying him. She did as he asked, and the removal of the tray revealed a swelling arousal tenting the wool blanket that covered him from the waist down.

She ran her hand over it, rewarded by the way his breath caught at her touch.

He slid down from his sitting position to lie flat on the bed, then flung away the blanket. He was naked but for the bandages, and a pleased thrill ran through her at the sight of him, body still undeniably powerful despite his wounds.

"Come here." He guided her forward until she straddled his hips, careful as she could not to jostle his leg. His stiffening cock pressed against her center, and she slid herself against it, but the fabric of her dress was in the way.

"Take off your dress."

Again, she obeyed, and the linen fabric fluttered to the floor atop the discarded blanket. His hands grasped her hips, pulling her against him. He probably shouldn't be gripping her that way with his injured left hand, but she wasn't about to tell him to stop.

"Remember that time you bound my wrists?" he murmured.

She glanced up at the hook on the wall where she'd secured him. The surrounding plaster was still cracked from their exploits. "Yes."

"I warned you I could free myself easily enough. But you didn't care. You said I'd let it hold me, because you wanted it that way."

Heat rushed through her at the memory of that coupling, one of their first. "I remember."

"This is going to be like that, understand? You're going to do as I ask, not because I'm compelling you, but because you want to please me. You do, don't you?"

"Yes," she sighed. Each word he spoke drove her arousal higher, like breaths coaxing a spark into a blaze.

"Good." He released his grasp on her hips. "Now sit on my face, Velia."

She hastened to comply, but when she settled herself over him, facing the wall behind his head, he tapped her hip. "Turn around."

Intrigued, she turned, so she faced the long sprawl of his body instead. It was a much more pleasant view, especially the stiff jut of his cock.

Her hips sank down onto his face, and she moaned as his mouth found her. He tongued her entrance, lapping at the wetness that had gathered, then moved higher. His lips fastened around the spot that begged for attention the most, and she sighed with pleasure.

He pulled his mouth away. "If there was one reason I wasn't afraid of dying, it's because I knew any half-decent version of Elysium would have to contain this." His muffled words vibrated against her. Then he took her between his lips once more.

She arched her back, leaning forward as she experimented to find the best angle in this new position. Then, with a pleasurable jolt, she realized—if she stretched even farther forward, bringing her body over his, she could reach his cock.

She did exactly that, bracing her hands on either side of his hips. She bent her head down and took him into her mouth.

He groaned against her. "Good girl," he grunted.

She realized this was what he intended with this position, only he'd waited for her to figure it out for herself.

Velia feared she wasn't very adept at doing it this way; she kept breaking off every time he did something particularly *good* with his mouth, losing focus, too consumed by the pleasure he was giving her. Then she noticed that every time she stopped, he did too. So she had to keep her mouth on him, had to keep her lips working, to fight through the pleasure that threatened to overwhelm her.

Even when the climax swiftly crashed over her, she kept her lips wrapped around him, her moans stifled on his cock.

When it passed, he lifted her hips off his face. "Take me inside you." His voice was hoarse with urgency.

She quickly swiveled around, shifting down his body, and notched him at her entrance. His attentions had made her slick, ready for him, and he slid inside with little resistance.

His eyes squeezed shut as she took him all the way to the hilt. "Ride me," he rasped.

It was the most unnecessary command he could have given, for her hips were already in motion. But she still thrilled to hear the rough, gravelly words. She leaned forward, taking him even deeper, and settled her hands on the mattress on either side of his head. His uninjured hand reached up to capture a breast, thumb sliding over her sensitized nipple. Her quim twitched with residual pleasure.

She found the rhythm he liked, a slow, deep rolling of her hips, and kept it up as his breathing grew more and more ragged. He raised his good hand to slide up her chest, taking gentle hold of her throat.

She kept rolling her hips, driving him closer and closer to his release, then lowered her head to kiss him. His fingers, still on her throat, twitched as her lips brushed his. She nipped his bottom lip, which drew a groan from his chest. Then she dragged her mouth down his neck, giving him a few more playful nibbles, before sinking her teeth into the muscled juncture of his shoulder.

His body went rigid, and his grip on her neck tightened for one brief, heady moment, fingers digging into her skin. Then he ripped his hand away. It flew down to grasp her hip, holding her against him as he shuddered. "Fuck, Velia," he ground out.

She soothed the sting of her bite with a kiss, her lips gentling as his body stilled.

Moments later, she lay tucked against his chest, head carefully positioned to avoid any wounds. His hand stroked her back in lazy passes. She expected him to succumb to sleep after the day he'd had, but after a brief silence, he spoke.

"In case it needs to be said, I'd marry you tomorrow. Or never, if that's what you wanted. I hadn't truly thought of getting married, having children. But with you…" Ferox gave a small shrug that jostled her head. "Everything seems possible."

She smiled. "I think the answer may be somewhere between tomorrow and never." His mention of children filled her with uncertainty, but she sensed the day might come when she'd relish the thought of being his wife and bearing his children. "For now, all I want is this. You." She ran a tender hand over his chest, skimming the old scars and new wounds, coming to rest atop his heart.

He covered her hand with his own. "Good. Because I'm yours, Velia. It doesn't matter if a priest declares it before the gods, or if no one but the two of us ever knows."

She laced her fingers with his, grinning. "You know the entire ludus knows about us, right? It's a bit too late for the latter option."

He chuckled. "So be it."

For her part, she was glad for people to know. She wanted to shout from the rooftops that Ferox was hers, to paint it on every wall in the city. *He's mine.* This stoic, fierce, protective man who bought three rugs and replaced her broken jug and trained her novice and safeguarded the ties to her hair and pleasured her until she couldn't think…he was all hers. A year ago, she might have scoffed at the thought of wanting one person for the rest of her life, but now, she could imagine nothing better than waking up next to him every day.

Well, perhaps one thing better: if she woke up with him each morning, that meant going to bed with him every night. And for *that* future? She couldn't wait.

Thank you for reading! Want more of Velia and Ferox? Scan below or head to **jennabigelow.com/gladiatorsembrace** for a steamy epilogue.

Don't miss Book 2, *Gladiator's Beloved*, which follows Ferox's friend Lea as she finds love with a certain "devastatingly hand-some" imperial physician…

Author's Note

THE IDEA FOR THIS book came from an anecdote recounted by Suetonius: future emperor Tiberius offered retired gladiators 100,000 sestertii each to return to the arena for one display of games. I used that figure to inspire the offer Ferox receives at the start of this book. It's difficult to equate ancient money to modern-day values, but from several estimates I've seen, it would certainly be equivalent to a six figure sum today (one estimate even put it in the seven figure range!). It was roughly what a highly educated and skilled man could earn in a year, and was many times more than a "normal" fee for a single gladiator's appearance.

Ferox's fighting record at the start of the book (twenty wins, eight draws, and four losses) is inspired by that of Flamma, a famous gladiator of Syrian descent whose record is immortalized on his tombstone as twenty-one wins, nine draws, and four losses. Flamma was offered his freedom multiple times, yet refused. He died at the age of thirty.

A common belief about gladiatorial combat is that a "thumbs up" at the end of a match indicates mercy, and "thumbs down" means death. In fact, the exact hand gestures are subject to debate. The Latin phrase used by Juvenal to describe the gesture for death is *verso pollice*, best translated as "with a turned thumb." I have chosen to be intentionally vague in my descriptions of the gesture, referring to it as a "thumb-out gesture," with a closed fist signaling mercy, so as not to perpetuate the thumbs up/thumbs down myth.

Another common misconception about gladiators is that they were all enslaved. Volunteer gladiators are well-documented. It's suggested that there may have been a roughly even split between enslaved and volunteer gladiators at times.

The biggest liberty I've taken is, of course, the idea of a woman managing gladiators. Women did run businesses, but as far as I know, there are no accounts of women managing gladiators as Velia aspires to do. If you're interested in how women fit into the world of gladiators, I hope you'll enjoy the next book in this series, which follows Penthesilea, a female gladiator, as she fights for her own happily ever after.

For further non-fiction reading, the main secondary source I consulted was *Gladiators and Caesars: The Power of Spectacle in Ancient Rome,* edited by Eckhart Kohne and Cornelia Ewigleben.

ACKNOWLEDGMENTS

A heartfelt thank you to the historical romance author community at large for inspiring and supporting me as a writer. I've learned so much from all of you, whether I'm lurking on your Threads posts or sliding into your Discord DMs.

Thank you to fellow authors Anne Knight and Dina S. for their insight on earlier drafts of this story, and to Emily Keyes for her editorial vision.

As always, thank you to Frankie, my husband and most enthusiastic reader. Listening to him cackle under his breath while reading my work is one of my greatest pleasures as an author.

ALSO BY JENNA BIGELOW

THE IMPERIAL GAMES SERIES

Set in the early days of Caligula's reign, the Imperial Games series follows three gladiators during a stretch of games held to celebrate the new emperor's accession. Win or lose, one thing is sure: love will be found where they least expect it.

Gladiator's Embrace (Book 1)

A retired gladiator reluctantly returns to the arena for one last series of fights, only to fall for his manager's ambitious niece when she hires him to train the up-and-coming gladiator she's taken on.

Gladiator's Beloved (Book 2)

She's Rome's most feared female gladiator. He's the emperor's personal physician, commanded to heal her latest injury. Sparks fly when they're together, until the machinations of the imperial court threaten to tear them apart.

Gladiator's Touch (Book 3)

A former Vestal Virgin seeks out the gladiator-turned-sculptor whose life she spared. He wants nothing to do with her after she ended his fighting career, but the heat that blossoms between them is impossible to escape.

THE ROMAN HEIRS SERIES

The Roman Heirs series follows the love stories of three generations of an unconventional family in the last decades of the Roman Republic. There's a politically motivated marriage of convenience, forbidden pining between a soldier and a governor's wife, and a pair of business rivals who somehow find themselves trading sex lessons for a truce.

The Merchant Match (prequel novella)

After gaining her freedom from slavery, Gaia will do whatever it takes to build a new future for herself and her son—even infiltrate a dinner party under an assumed identity to extort money from her former mistress. There, she meets Herminius, a wealthy merchant in search of a respectable bride. Despite her subterfuge, Gaia can't ignore the heat that sparks between them. She knows she should keep her distance, but what's the point of freedom if she can't enjoy the pleasurable attentions of a man who makes her heart flutter every time they touch?

The Tribune Temptation (Book 1)

In the cutthroat world of Roman politics, family is everything. Aelius, a freed slave turned ambitious politician, enters into a marriage of convenience with a disgraced patrician divorcee, hoping her powerful family name will bolster his chances in his next election. Prickly one moment and icy the next, Crispina is determined to keep her charming husband at a distance. That is, until Aelius undertakes a campaign to win not just the city's vote, but his wife's heart.

The Legionary Seduction (Book 2)

Max joined the Roman army in search of glory and adventure, but soon finds himself stuck in the provinces, unable to land even one promotion. During a stint on guard duty at the new governor's residence, he comes face-to-face with Volusia, the girl he loved ten years ago. Only now, she's married to the governor. But when her husband mysteriously dies and she suspects foul play, the only person Volusia dares trust is Max, and she begs him to help investigate. Their love is strong, but can it withstand a killer's blade?

The Fortune Flirtation (Book 3)

After losing her husband to a shipwreck, Lucretia has devoted herself to keeping his shipping business afloat. Felix, her scheming rival, strives for a monopoly on trade, which requires seizing Lucretia's ships for himself. Unfortunately for Felix, it's not just her ships he desires. Even worse, he's been too busy building his business empire to dally with women…*ever*. When Lucretia discovers both how much he wants her *and* that he's as inexperienced as a Vestal Virgin, she decides to use this to her advantage—proposing a truce in exchange for initiating Felix into the ways of the flesh.

OTHER WORKS

A Princess's Ransom (Tales of Timeless Romance anthology)

After the sack of Rome, Galla Placidia, the emperor's sister, becomes the Goths' most valuable hostage. While awaiting ransom, the ambitious princess, tired of living in her brother's shadow, realizes the Goths could be the key to the power she craves. Allying with the Goths could also allow her to indulge her forbidden attraction to her captor—the stoic, noble, and irritatingly handsome Athaulf. Placidia must decide how far she'll go to secure both the man and the future she desires, and if she's willing to turn her back on Rome forever.

About the Author

Jenna Bigelow is a historical romance author based in Wilmington, DE. She has eleven years of Latin classes under her belt, as well as a minor in Classical Culture and Society. When not writing, she enjoys sewing, especially recreating historical fashions of the 18th and 19th centuries. She thinks about the Roman Empire every day.

Connect with Jenna at her website, jennabigelow.com, or on Instagram/Threads at @jennabigelowwrites.